TRAILING WEST

Center Point
Large Print

**This Large Print Book carries the
Seal of Approval of N.A.V.H.**

TRAILING WEST
A Western Quartet

LOUIS L'AMOUR

edited by
JON TUSKA

A Circle Ⓥ Western

CENTER POINT PUBLISHING
THORNDIKE, MAINE

This Circle V Western is published by
Center Point Large Print in the year 2008
in cooperation with Golden West Literary Agency.

Copyright © 2008 by Golden West Literary Agency.

The text of this Large Print edition is unabridged. In other
aspects, this book may vary from the original edition.
Printed in the United States of America.
Set in 16-point Times New Roman type.

ISBN: 978-1-60285-121-4

Cataloging-in-Publication data is available from the Library of Congress.

Acknowledgments

"Trap of Gold" first appeared in *Argosy* (8/51). Copyright © 1951 by Popular Publications, Inc. Copyright not renewed.

"Keep Travelin', Rider" under the byline Jim Mayo first appeared in *Thrilling Western* (2/48). Copyright © 1948 by Standard Magazines, Inc. Copyright not renewed.

"Dutchman's Flat" first appeared in *Giant Western* (Fall, 48). Copyright © 1948 by Best Publications, Inc. Copyright not renewed.

"The Rider of Lost Creek" under the byline Jim Mayo first appeared in *West* (4/47). Copyright © 1947 by Better Publications, Inc. Copyright not renewed.

TABLE OF CONTENTS

Introduction
by Jon Tuska

Louis Dearborn LaMoore (1908-1988) was born in Jamestown, North Dakota. He left home at fifteen and subsequently held a wide variety of jobs although he worked mostly as a merchant seaman. From his earliest youth, L'Amour had a love of verse. His first published work was a poem, "The Chap Worth While", appearing when he was eighteen years old in his former hometown's newspaper, the *Jamestown Sun*. It is the only poem from his early years that he left out of SMOKE FROM THIS ALTAR, which appeared in 1939 from Lusk Publishers in Oklahoma City, a book which L'Amour published himself; however, this poem is reproduced in THE LOUIS L'AMOUR COMPANION (Andrews and McMeel, 1992) edited by Robert Weinberg. L'Amour wrote poems and articles for a number of small circulation arts magazines all through the early 1930s and, after hundreds of rejection slips, finally had his first story accepted, "Anything for a Pal" in *True Gang Life* (10/35). He returned in 1938 to live with his family where they had settled in Choctaw, Oklahoma, determined to make writing his career. He wrote a fight story bought by Standard Magazines that year and became acquainted with editor Leo Margulies who was to play an important rôle later in L'Amour's life. "The Town No Guns Could Tame" in *New*

Western (3/40) was his first published Western story.

During the Second World War L'Amour was drafted and ultimately served with the U.S. Army Transportation Corps in Europe. However, in the two years before he was shipped out, he managed to write a great many adventure stories for Standard Magazines. The first story he published in 1946, the year of his discharge, was a Western, "Law of the Desert Born" in *Dime Western* (4/46). A call to Leo Margulies resulted in L'Amour's agreeing to write Western stories for the various Western pulp magazines published by Standard Magazines, a third of which appeared under the byline Jim Mayo, the name of a character in L'Amour's earlier adventure fiction. The proposal for L'Amour to write new Hopalong Cassidy novels came from Margulies who wanted to launch *Hopalong Cassidy's Western Magazine* to take advantage of the popularity William Boyd's old films and new television series were enjoying with a new generation. Doubleday & Company agreed to publish the pulp novelettes in hard cover books. L'Amour was paid $500 a story, no royalties, and he was assigned the house name Tex Burns. L'Amour read Clarence E. Mulford's books about the Bar-20 and based his Hopalong Cassidy on Mulford's original creation. Only two issues of the magazine appeared before it ceased publication. Doubleday felt that the Hopalong character had to appear exactly as William Boyd did in the films and on television and thus even the first two novels had to be revamped to meet with this requirement prior to publication in book form.

L'Amour's first Western novel under his own byline was WESTWARD THE TIDE (World's Work, 1950). It was rejected by every American publisher to which it was submitted. World's Work paid a flat £75 without royalties for British Empire rights in perpetuity. L'Amour sold his first Western short story to a slick magazine a year later, "The Gift of Cochise" in *Collier's* (7/5/52). Robert Fellows and John Wayne purchased screen rights to this story from L'Amour for $4,000 and James Edward Grant, one of Wayne's favorite screenwriters, developed a script from it, changing L'Amour's Ches Lane to Hondo Lane. L'Amour retained the right to novelize Grant's screenplay, which differs substantially from his short story, and he was able to get an endorsement from Wayne to be used as a blurb, stating that HONDO was the finest Western Wayne had ever read. HONDO (Fawcett Gold Medal, 1953) by Louis L'Amour was released on the same day as the film, HONDO (Warner, 1953), with a first printing of 320,000 copies.

With SHOWDOWN AT YELLOW BUTTE (Ace, 1953) by Jim Mayo, L'Amour began a series of short Western novels for Don Wollheim that could be doubled with other short novels by other authors in Ace Publishing's paperback two-fers. Advances on these were $800 and usually the author never earned any royalties. HELLER WITH A GUN (Fawcett Gold Medal, 1955) was the first of a series of original

Westerns L'Amour had agreed to write under his own name following the success for Fawcett of HONDO. L'Amour wanted even this early to have his Western novels published in hard cover editions. He expanded "Guns of the Timberland" by Jim Mayo in *West* (9/50) for GUNS OF THE TIMBERLANDS (Jason Press, 1955), a hard cover Western for which he was paid an advance of $250. Another novel for Jason Press followed and then SILVER CAÑON (Avalon Books, 1956) for Thomas Bouregy & Company. These were basically lending library publishers and the books seldom earned much money above the small advances paid.

The great turn in L'Amour's fortunes came about because of problems Saul David was having with his original paperback Westerns program at Bantam Books. Fred Glidden had been signed to a contract to produce two original paperback Luke Short Western novels a year for an advance of $15,000 each. It was a long-term contract but, in the first ten years of it, Fred only wrote six novels. Literary agent Marguerite Harper then persuaded Bantam that Fred's brother, Jon, could help fulfill the contract and Jon was signed for eight Peter Dawson Western novels. When Jon died suddenly before completing even one book for Bantam, Harper managed to engage a ghost writer at the Disney studios to write these eight "Peter Dawson" novels, beginning with THE SAVAGES (Bantam, 1959). They proved inferior to anything Jon had ever written and what sales they had seemed to be due only to the Peter Dawson name.

Saul David wanted to know from L'Amour if *he* could deliver two Western novels a year. L'Amour said he could, and he did. In fact, by 1962 this number was increased to three original paperback novels a year. The first L'Amour novel to appear under the Bantam contract was RADIGAN (Bantam, 1958). It seemed to me after I read all of the Western stories L'Amour ever wrote in preparation for my essay, "Louis L'Amour's Western Fiction" in A VARIABLE HARVEST (McFarland, 1990), that by the time L'Amour wrote "Riders of the Dawn" in *Giant Western* (6/51), the short novel he later expanded to form SILVER CAÑON, that he had almost burned out on the Western story, and this was years before his fame, wealth, and tremendous sales figures. He had developed seven basic plot situations in his pulp Western stories and he used them over and over again in writing his original paperback Westerns. FLINT (Bantam, 1960), considered by many to be one of L'Amour's better efforts, is basically a reprise of the range war plot which, of the seven, is the one L'Amour used most often. L'Amour's hero, Flint, knows about a hide-out in the badlands (where, depending on the story, something is hidden: cattle, horses, outlaws, etc.). Even certain episodes within his basic plots are repeated again and again. Flint scales a sharp V in a cañon wall to escape a tight spot as Jim Gatlin had before him in L'Amour's "The Black Rock Coffin Makers" in *.44 Western* (2/50) and many a L'Amour hero would again.

Basic to this range war plot is the villain's means for crowding out the other ranchers in a district. He brings in a giant herd that requires all the available grass and forces all the smaller ranchers out of business. It was this same strategy Bantam used in marketing L'Amour. *All* of his Western titles were continuously kept in print. Independent distributors were required to buy titles in lots of 10,000 copies if they wanted access to other Bantam titles at significantly discounted prices. In time L'Amour's paperbacks forced almost every one else off the racks in the Western sections. L'Amour himself comprised the other half of this successful strategy. He dressed up in cowboy outfits, traveled about the country in a motor home visiting with independent distributors, taking them to dinner and charming them, making them personal friends. He promoted himself at every available opportunity. L'Amour insisted that he was telling the stories of the people who had made America a great nation and he appealed to patriotism as much as to commercialism in his rhetoric.

His fiction suffered, of course, stories written hurriedly and submitted in their first draft and published as he wrote them. A character would have a rifle in his hand, a model not yet invented in the period in which the story was set, and when he crossed a street the rifle would vanish without explanation. A scene would begin in a saloon and suddenly the setting would be a hotel dining room. Characters would die once and, a few pages later, die again. An old man for most of a story would turn out to be in his twenties.

Once when we were talking and Louis had showed me his topographical maps and his library of thousands of volumes which he claimed he used for research, he asserted that, if he claimed there was a rock in a road at a certain point in a story, his readers knew that if they went to that spot they would find the rock just as he described it. I told him that might be so but I personally was troubled by the many inconsistencies in his stories. Take LAST STAND AT PAPAGO WELLS (Fawcett Gold Medal, 1957). Five characters are killed during an Indian raid. One of the surviving characters emerges from seclusion after the attack and counts *six* corpses.

"I'll have to go back and count them again," L'Amour said, and smiled. "But, you know, I don't think the people who read my books would really care."

All of this notwithstanding, there are many fine, and some spectacular, moments in Louis L'Amour's Western fiction. I think he was at his best in the shorter forms, especially his magazine stories, and the two best stories he ever wrote appeared in the 1950s, "The Gift of Cochise" early in the decade and "War Party" in *The Saturday Evening Post* (6/59). The latter was later expanded by L'Amour to serve as the opening chapters for BENDIGO SHAFTER (Dutton, 1979). That book is so poorly structured that Harold Kuebler, senior editor at Doubleday & Company to whom it was first offered, said he would not publish it unless L'Amour undertook extensive revisions. This L'Amour refused to do and, eventually, Bantam started a hard cover publishing program to accommodate him when no other hard cover publisher proved willing to accept his books as he wrote them. Yet "War Party" possesses several of the characteristics in purest form which I suspect, no matter how diluted they ultimately would become, account in largest measure for the loyal following Louis L'Amour won from his readers: the young male narrator who is in the process of growing into manhood and who is evaluating other human beings and his own experiences; a resourceful frontier woman who has beauty as well as fortitude; a strong male character who is single and hence marriageable; and the powerful, romantic, strangely compelling vision of the American West which invests L'Amour's Western fiction and makes it such a delightful escape from the cares of a later time—in this author's words from this story, that "big country needing big men and women to live in it" and where there was no place for "the frightened or the mean."

TRAILING WEST
A Western Quartet

Trap of Gold

Wetherton had been three months out of Horsehead before he found his first color. At first, it was a few scattered grains taken from the base of an alluvial fan where millions of tons of sand and silt had washed down from a chain of rugged peaks; yet the gold was ragged under the magnifying glass.

Gold that has carried any distance becomes worn and polished by the abrasive action of the accompanying rocks and sand, so this could not have been carried far. With caution born of harsh experience, he seated himself and lit his pipe, yet excitement was strong within him.

A contemplative man by nature, his experience had taught him how a man may be deluded by hope, yet all his instincts told him the source of the gold was somewhere on the mountain above. It could have come down the wash that skirted the base of the mountain, but the ragged condition of the gold made that improbable.

The base of the fan was a half mile across and hundreds of feet thick, built of silt and sand washed down by centuries of erosion among the higher peaks. The point of the wide V of the fan lay between two towering upthrusts of granite, but from where Wetherton sat, he could see that the actual source of the fan lay much higher.

Wetherton made camp near a tiny spring west of the

fan, then picketed his burros and began his climb. When he was well over 2,000 feet higher, he stopped, resting again, and, while resting, he dry-panned some of the silt. Surprisingly there were more than a few grains of gold even in that first pan, so he continued his climb and passed at last between the towering portals of the granite columns.

Above this natural gate were three smaller alluvial fans that joined at the gate to pour into the greater fan below. Dry-panning two of these brought no results, but the third, even by the relatively poor method of dry-panning, showed a dozen colors, all of good size.

The head of this fan lay in a gigantic crack in a granite upthrust that resembled a fantastic ruin. Pausing to catch his breath, he let his gaze wander along the base of this upthrust, and right before him the crumbling granite was slashed with a vein of quartz that was literally laced with gold!

Struggling nearer through the loose sand, his heart pounding more from excitement than from altitude and exertion, he came to an abrupt stop. The band of quartz was six feet wide, and that six feet was cob-webbed with gold.

It was unbelievable, but there it was.

Yet even in this moment of success, something about the beetling cliff stopped him from going forward. His innate caution took hold, and he drew back to examine it at greater length. Wary of what he saw, he circled the batholith, and then climbed to the ridge behind it, from which he could look down upon the roof. What he saw from there left him dry-mouthed and jittery.

The granite upthrust was obviously a part of a much older range, one that had weathered and worn, suffered from shock and twisting, until finally this tower of granite had been violently upthrust, leaving it standing, a shaky ruin among younger and sturdier peaks. In the process, the rock had been shattered and riven by mighty forces until it had become a miner's horror. Wetherton stared, fascinated by the prospect. With enormous wealth there for the taking, every ounce must be taken at the risk of life.

One stick of powder might bring the whole crumbling mass down in a heap, and it loomed all of 300 feet above its base in the fan. The roof of the batholith was riven with gigantic cracks, literally seamed with breaks like the wall of an ancient building that has remained standing after heavy bombing. Walking back to the base of the tower, Wetherton found he could actually break loose chunks of the quartz with his fingers.

The vein itself lay on the downhill side and at the very base. The outer wall of the upthrust was sharply tilted so that a man working at the vein would be cutting his way into the very foundations of the tower, and any single blow of the pick might bring the whole mass down upon him. Furthermore, if the rock did fall, the vein would be hopelessly buried under thousands of tons of rock and lost without the expenditure of much more capital than he could command. And at this moment, Wetherton's total of money in hand amounted to slightly less than $40.

Thirty yards from the face, he seated himself upon the sand and filled his pipe once more. A man might take tons out of there without trouble, and yet it might collapse at the first blow. He knew he had no choice. He needed money, and it lay there before him. Even if he were at first successful, there were two things he must avoid. The first was tolerance of danger that might bring carelessness; the second, that urge to go back for that little bit more that could kill him.

It was well into the afternoon, and he had not eaten, yet he was not hungry. He circled the batholith, studying it from every angle, only to reach the conclusion that his first estimate had been correct. The only way to get to the gold was to go into the very shadow of the leaning wall and attack it at its base, digging it out by main strength. From where he stood, it seemed ridiculous that a mere man with a pick could topple that mass of rock, yet he knew how delicate such a balance could be.

The tower was situated on what might be described as the military crest of the ridge, and the alluvial fan sloped steeply away from its lower side, steeper than a steep stairway. The top of the leaning wall overshadowed the top of the fan, and, if it started to crumble and a man had warning, he might run to the north with a bare chance of escape. The soft sand in which he must run would be an impediment, but that could be alleviated by making a walk from flat rocks sunken into the sand.

It was dusk when he returned to his camp. Deliberately he had not permitted himself to begin work, not by so much as a sample. He must be deliberate in all his actions, and never for a second should he forget the mass that towered above him. A split second of hesitation when the crash came—and he accepted it as inevitable—would mean burial under tons of crumbled rock.

The following morning, he picketed his burros on a small meadow near the spring, cleaned the spring itself, and prepared a lunch. Then he removed his shirt, drew on a pair of gloves, and walked to the face of the cliff. Yet even then he did not begin, knowing that upon this habit of care and deliberation might depend not only his success in the venture but life itself. He gathered flat stones and began building his walk. *When you start moving*, he told himself, *you'll have to be fast.*

Finally, and with infinite care, he began tapping at the quartz, enlarging cracks with the pick, removing fragments, then prying loose whole chunks. He did not swing the pick but used it as a lever. The quartz was rotten, and a man might obtain a considerable amount by this method of picking or even pulling with the hands. When he had a sack filled with the richest quartz, he carried it over his path to a safe place beyond the shadow of the tower. Returning, he tamped a few more flat rocks into his path and began on the second sack. He worked with greater care than was, perhaps, essential. He was not and had never been a gambling man.

In the present operation, he was taking a carefully calculated risk in which every eventuality had been weighed and judged. He needed the money, and he intended to have it; he had a good idea of his chances of success, but knew that his gravest danger was to become too greedy, too much engrossed in his task.

Dragging the two sacks down the hill, he found a flat block of stone and with a singlejack proceeded to break up the quartz. It was a slow and hard job, but he had no better means of extracting the gold. After breaking or crushing the quartz, much of the gold could be separated by a knife blade, for it was amazingly concentrated. With water from the spring, Wetherton panned the remainder until it was too dark to see.

Out of his blankets by daybreak, he ate breakfast and completed the extraction of the gold. At a rough estimate, his first day's work would run to $400. He made a cache for the gold sack and took the now-empty ore sacks and climbed back to the tower.

The air was clear and fresh, the sun warm after the chill of night, and he liked the feel of the pick in his hands.

Laura and Tommy awaited him back in Horsehead, and, if he was killed here, there was small chance they would ever know what had become of him. But he did not intend to be killed. The gold he was extracting from this rock was for them and not for himself.

It would mean an easier life in a larger town, a home of their own, and the things to make the home a woman desires. And it meant an education for Tommy. For himself all he needed was the thought of that home to return to, his wife and son—and the desert itself. And one was as necessary to him as the other.

The desert would be the death of him. He had been told that many times and did not need to be told, for few men knew the desert as he did. The desert was to him what an orchestra is to a fine conductor, what the human body is to a surgeon. It was his work, his life, and the thing he knew best. He always smiled when he looked first into the desert as he started a new trip. Would this be it?

The morning drew on, and he continued to work with an even-paced swing of the pick, a careful filling of the sack. The gold showed bright and beautiful in the crystalline quartz, which was so much more beautiful than the gold itself. From time to time as the morning drew on, he paused to rest and to breathe deeply of the fresh, clear air. Deliberately he refused to hurry.

For nineteen days, he worked tirelessly, eight hours a day at first, then lessening his hours to seven, and then to six. Wetherton did not explain to himself why he did this, but he realized it was becoming increasingly difficult to stay on the job. Again and again, he would walk away from the rock face on one excuse or another, and each time he would begin to feel his scalp prickle, his steps grow quicker, and each time he returned more reluctantly.

Three times, beginning on the 13th, again on the 17th, and finally on the 19th day, he heard movement within the tower. Whether that whispering in the rock was normal he did not know. Such a natural movement might have been going on for centuries. He only knew that it happened then, and each time it happened, a cold chill went along his spine.

His work had cut a deep notch at the base of the tower, such a notch as a man might make in felling a tree, but wider and deeper. The sacks of gold, too, were increasing. They now numbered seven, and their total would, he believed, amount to more than $5,000—probably nearer to $6,000. As he cut deeper into the rock, the vein was growing richer.

He worked on his knees now. The vein had slanted downward as he cut into the base of the tower, and he was all of nine feet into the rock with the great mass of it above him. If that rock gave way while he was working, he would be crushed in an instant, with no chance of escape. Nevertheless, he continued.

The change in the rock tower was not the only change, for he had lost weight, and he no longer slept well. On the night of the 20th day, he decided he had

$6,000 and his goal would be $10,000. And the following day, the rock was the richest ever! As if to tantalize him into working on and on, the deeper he cut, the richer the ore became. By nightfall of that day, he had taken out more than $1,000.

Now the lust for the gold was getting into him, taking him by the throat. He was fascinated by the danger of the tower as well as the desire for the gold. Three more days to go—could he leave it then? He looked again at the tower and felt a peculiar sense of foreboding, a feeling that here he was to die, that he would never escape. Was it his imagination, or had the outer wall leaned a little more?

On the morning of the 22nd day, he climbed the fan over a path that use had built into a series of continuous steps. He had never counted those steps, but there must have been over 1,000 of them. Dropping his canteen into a shaded hollow and pick in hand, he started for the tower.

The forward tilt *did* seem somewhat more than before. Or was it the light? The crack that ran behind the outer wall seemed to have widened, and, when he examined it more closely, he found a small pile of freshly run silt near the bottom of the crack. So it had moved!

Wetherton hesitated, staring at the rock with wary attention. He was a fool to go back in there again. $7,000 was more than he had ever had in his life before, yet in the next few hours he could take out at least $1,000 more, and in the next three days he could easily have the $10,000 he had set for his goal.

He walked to the opening, dropped to his knees, and crawled into the narrowing, flat-roofed hole. No sooner was he inside than fear climbed up into his throat. He felt trapped, stifled, but he fought down the mounting panic and began to work. His first blows were so frightened and feeble that nothing came loose. Yet when he did get started, he began to work with a feverish intensity that was wholly unlike him.

When he slowed, and then stopped to fill his sack, he was gasping for breath, but despite his hurry, the sack was not quite full. Reluctantly he lifted his pick again, but before he could strike a blow, the gigantic mass above him seemed to *creak* like something tired and old. A deep shudder went through the colossal pile, and then a deep grinding that turned him sick with horror. All his plans for instant flight were frozen, and it was not until the groaning ceased that he realized he was lying on his back, breathless with fear and expectancy. Slowly he edged his way into the air and walked, fighting the desire to run away from the rock.

When he stopped near his canteen, he was wringing with cold sweat and trembling in every muscle. He sat down on the rock and fought for control. It was not until some twenty minutes had passed that he could trust himself to get to his feet.

Despite his experience, he knew that, if he did not go back now, he would never go. He had taken out but one sack for the day and wanted another. Circling the batholith, he examined the widening crack, endeavoring again, for the third time, to find another means of access to the vein.

The tilt of the outer wall was obvious, and it could stand no more without toppling. It was possible that by cutting into the wall of the column and striking down, he might tap the vein at a safer point. Yet this added blow at the foundation would bring the tower nearer to collapse and render his other hole untenable. Even this new attempt would not be safe, although immeasurably more secure than the hole he had left. Hesitating, he looked back at the hole.

Once more? The ore was now fabulously rich, and the few pounds he needed to complete the sack he could get in just a little while. He stared at the black and undoubtedly narrower hole, then looked up at the leaning wall. He picked up his pick and, his mouth dry, started back, drawn by a fascination that was beyond all reason.

His heart pounding, he dropped to his knees at the tunnel face. The air seemed stifling, and he could feel his scalp tingling, but once he started to crawl, it was better. The face where he now worked was at least sixteen feet from the tunnel mouth. Pick in hand, he began to wedge chunks from their seat. The going seemed harder now, and the chunks did not come loose so easily. Above him, the tower made no sound. The crushing weight was now something tangible. He could almost feel it growing, increasing with every move of his. The mountain seemed resting on his shoulder, crushing the air from his lungs.

Suddenly he stopped. His sack almost full, he stopped and lay very still, staring up at the bulk of the rock above him.

No.

He would go no farther. Now he would quit. Not another sackful. Not another pound. He would go out now. He would go down the mountain without a backward look, and he would keep going. His wife waiting at home, little Tommy, who would run gladly to meet him—these were too much to gamble.

With the decision came peace, came certainty. He sighed deeply and relaxed, and then it seemed to him that every muscle in his body had been knotted with strain. He turned on his side and with great deliberation gathered his lantern, his sack, his hand pick.

He had won. He had defeated the crumbling tower; he had defeated his own greed. He backed easily, without the caution that had marked his earlier movements in the cave. His blind, trusting foot found the projecting rock, a piece of quartz that stuck out from the rough-hewn wall.

The blow was too weak, too feeble to have brought forth the reaction that followed. The rock seemed to quiver like the flesh of a beast when stabbed; a queer vibration went through that ancient rock, then a deep, gasping sigh.

He had waited too long!

Fear came swiftly in upon him, crowding him,

while his body twisted, contracting into the smallest possible space. He tried to will his muscles to move beneath the growing sounds that vibrated through the passage. The whispers of the rock grew into a terrifying groan, and there was a *rattle* of pebbles. Then silence.

The silence was more horrifying than the sound. Somehow he was crawling, even as he expected the avalanche of gold to bury him. Abruptly his feet were in the open. He was out.

He ran without stopping, but behind him he heard a growing roar that he couldn't outrace. When he knew from the slope of the land that he must be safe from falling rock, he fell to his knees. He turned and looked back. The muted, roaring sound, like thunder beyond mountains, continued, but there was no visible change in the tower. Suddenly, as he watched, the whole rock formation seemed to shift and tip. The movement lasted only seconds, but before the tons of rock had found their new equilibrium, his tunnel and the area around it had utterly vanished from sight.

When he could finally stand, Wetherton gathered up his sack of ore and his canteen. The wind was cool upon his face as he walked away, and he did not look back again.

Keep Travelin', Rider

I

When Tack Gentry sighted the weather-beaten buildings of the G Bar, he touched spurs to the buckskin
and the horse broke into a fast canter that carried the
cowhand down the trail and around into the ranch
yard. He swung down.

"Hey!" he yelled happily, grinning. "Is that all the
welcome I get?"

The door pushed open and a man stepped out on the
worn porch. The man had a stubble of beard and a
drooping mustache. His blue eyes were small and
narrow.

"Who are you?" he demanded. "And what do you
want?"

"I'm Tack Gentry," Tack said. "Where's Uncle John?"

"I don't know you," the man said, "and I never
heard of no Uncle John. I reckon you got onto the
wrong spread, youngster."

"Wrong spread?" Tack laughed. "Quit your
funnin'! I helped build that house there, and built the
corrals by my lonesome, while Uncle John was sick.
Where is everybody?"

The man looked at him carefully and then lifted his
eyes to a point beyond Tack. A voice spoke from
behind the cowhand. "Reckon you been gone a while,
ain't you?"

Gentry turned. The man behind him was short, stocky, and blond. He had a wide, flat face, a small broken nose, and cruel eyes.

"Gone? I reckon, yes. I've been gone most of a year. Went north with a trail herd to Ellsworth, then took me a job as *segundo* on a herd movin' to Wyoming."

Tack stared around, his eyes alert and curious. There was something wrong here, something very wrong. The neatness that had been typical of Uncle John Gentry was gone. The place looked run-down, the porch was untidy, the door hung loosely on its hinges, even the horses in the corral were different.

"Where's Uncle John?" Tack demanded again. "Quit stallin'!"

The blond man smiled, his lips parting over broken teeth and a hard, cynical light coming into his eyes. "If you mean John Gentry, who used to live on this place, he's gone. He drawed on the wrong man and got himself killed."

"What?" Tack's stomach felt like he had been kicked. He stood there, staring. "He *drew* on somebody? Uncle John?" Tack shook his head. "That's impossible. John Gentry was a Quaker. He never lifted a hand in violence against anybody or anything in his life. He never even wore a gun, never owned one."

"I only know what they tell me," the blond man said, "but we got work to do, and I reckon you better slope out of here. And," he added grimly, "if you're smart, you'll keep right on goin', clean out of the country!"

"What do you mean?" Tack's thoughts were in a turmoil, trying to accustom himself to this change, wondering what could have happened, what was behind it.

"I mean you'll find things considerably changed around here. If you decide not to leave," he added, "you might ride into Sunbonnet and look up Van Hardin or Dick Olney and tell him I said to give you all you had comin'. Tell 'em Soderman sent you."

"Who's Van Hardin?" Tack asked. The name was unfamiliar.

"You been away, all right," Soderman acknowledged. "Or you'd know who Van Hardin is. He runs this country. He's the ramrod, Hardin is. Olney's sheriff."

Tack Gentry rode away from his home ranch with his thoughts in confusion. Uncle John killed in a gun-fight? Why, that was out of reason! The old man wouldn't fight. He never had and never would. And this Dick Olney was sheriff! What had become of Pete Liscomb? No election was due for another year, and Pete had been a good sheriff.

There was one way to solve the problem and get the whole story, and that was to circle around and ride by the London Ranch. Bill could give him the whole story, and, besides, he wanted to see Betty. It had been a long time.

The six miles to the headquarters of the London Ranch went by swiftly, yet, as Tack rode, he scanned the grassy levels along the Maravillas. There were cattle enough, more than he had ever seen on the old G Bar, and all of them wearing the G Bar brand.

He reined in sharply. What the . . . ? Why, if Uncle John was dead, the ranch belonged to him! But if that was so, who was Soderman? And what were they doing on his ranch?

Three men were loafing on the wide verandah of the London ranch house when Tack rode up. All their faces were unfamiliar. He glanced warily from one to the other.

"Where's Bill London?" he asked.

"London?" The man in the wide brown hat shrugged. "Reckon he's to home, over in Sunbonnet Pass. He ain't never over here."

"This is his ranch, isn't it?" Tack demanded.

All three men seemed to tense. "His ranch?" The man in the brown hat shook his head. "Reckon you're a stranger around here. This ranch belongs to Van Hardin. London ain't got a ranch. Nothin' but a few acres back against the creek over to Sunbonnet Pass. He and that girl of his live there. I reckon, though,"— he grinned suddenly—"she won't be there much longer. Hear tell she's goin' to work in the Longhorn dance hall."

"Betty London? In the Longhorn?" Tack exclaimed. "Don't make me laugh, partner! Betty's too nice a girl for that! She wouldn't. . . ."

"They got it advertised," the brown-hatted man said calmly.

An hour later a very thoughtful Tack Gentry rode up the dusty street of Sunbonnet. In that hour of riding he had been doing a lot of thinking, and he was remembering what Soderman had said. He was to tell Hardin or Olney that Soderman had sent him to get all that was coming to him. Suddenly that remark took on a new significance.

Tack swung down in front of the Longhorn. Emblazoned on the front of the saloon was a huge poster announcing that Betty London was the coming attraction, that she would sing and entertain at the Longhorn. Compressing his lips, Tack walked into the saloon.

Nothing was familiar except the bar and the tables. The man behind the bar was squat and fat, and his eyes peered at Tack from folds of flesh. "What's it fur you?" he demanded.

"Rye," Tack said. He let his eyes swing slowly around the room. Not a familiar face greeted him. Shorty Davis was gone. Nick Farmer was not around. These men were strangers, a tight-mouthed, hard-eyed crew.

Gentry glanced at the bartender. "Any ridin' jobs around here? Driftin' through, and thought I might like to tie in with one of the outfits around here."

"Keep driftin'," the bartender said, not glancing at him. "Everybody's got a full crew."

One door swung open and a tall, clean-cut man walked into the room, glancing around. He wore a neat gray suit and a dark hat. Tack saw the bartender's eyes harden and glanced thoughtfully at the newcomer. The man's face was very thin, and, when he removed his hat, his ash blond hair was neatly combed.

He glanced around, and his eyes lighted on Tack. "Stranger?" he asked pleasantly. "Then may I buy you a drink? I don't like to drink alone, but haven't sunk so low as to drink with these coyotes."

Tack stiffened, expecting a reaction from some of the seated men, but there was none. Puzzled, he glanced at the blond man and, seeing the cynical good humor in the man's eyes, nodded. "Sure, I'll drink with you."

"My name," the tall man added, "is Anson Childe, by profession a lawyer, by dint of circumstances a gambler, and by choice a student. You perhaps wonder," he added, "why these men do not resent my reference to them as coyotes. There are three reasons, I expect. The first is that some subconscious sense of truth makes them appreciate the justice of the term. Second, they know I am gifted with considerable dexterity in expounding the gospel of Judge Colt. Third, they know that I am dying of tuberculosis and as a result have no fear of bullets. It is not exactly fear that keeps them from drawing on me. Let us say it is a matter of mathematics, and a problem none of them has succeeded in solving with any degree of comfort is the result. It is . . . how many of them would die before I did? You can appreciate, my friend, the quandary in which this places them, and also the disagreeable realization that bullets are no respecters of persons, nor am I. The several out there who might draw know that I know who they are. The result is that they know they would be first to die." Childe looked at Tack thoughtfully. "I heard you ask about a riding job as I came in. You look like an honest man, and there is no place here for such."

Gentry hunted for the right words. Then he said: "This country looks like it was settled by honest men."

Anson Childe studied his glass. "Yes," he said, "but at the right moment they lacked a leader. One was too opposed to violence, another was too law-abiding, and the rest lacked resolution."

If there was a friend in the community, this man was it. Tack finished his drink and strode to the door. The bartender met his eyes as he glanced back.

"Keep on driftin'," the bartender said.

Tack Gentry smiled. "I like it here," he said, "and I'm stayin'."

He swung into the saddle and turned his buckskin toward Sunbonnet Pass. He still had no idea exactly what had happened during the year of his absence, yet Childe's remark coupled with what the others had said told him a little. Apparently some strong, res-olute men had moved in and taken over, and there had been no concerted fight against them, no organiza-tion, and no leadership.

Childe had said that one was opposed to violence. That would have been his uncle John. The one who was too law-abiding would be Bill London. London had always been strong for law and order and settling things in a legal way. The others had been honest men, but small ranchers and individually unable to oppose whatever was done to them. Yet whatever had happened, the incoming elements had apparently moved with speed and finesse. Had it been one ranch, it would have been different. But the ranches and the town seemed completely subjugated.

The buckskin took the trail at an easy canter, skirting the long red cliff of Horse Thief Mesa and wading the creek at Gunsight. Sunbonnet Pass opened before him like a gate in the mountains. To the left, in a grove of trees, was a small adobe house and a corral.

Two horses were standing at the corral as he rode up. His eyes narrowed as he saw them. Button and Blackie! Two of his uncle's favorites and two horses he had raised from colts. He swung down and started toward them, when he saw the three people on the steps.

He turned to face them, and his heart jumped. Betty London had not changed.

Her eyes widened, and her face went dead white. "Tack!" she gasped. "Tack Gentry!"

Even as she spoke, Tack saw the sudden shock with which the two men turned to stare. "That's right, Betty," he said quietly. "I just got home."

"But . . . but . . . we heard you were dead!"

"I'm not." His eyes shifted to the two men—a thick-shouldered, deep-chested man with a square, swarthy face and a lean, raw-boned man wearing a star. The one with the star would be Dick Olney. The other must be Van Hardin.

Tack's eyes swung to Olney. "I heard my uncle John Gentry was killed. Did you investigate his death?"

Olney's eyes were careful. "Yeah," he said. "He was killed in a fair fight. Gun in his hand."

"My uncle," Tack replied, "was a Quaker. He never lifted a hand in violence in his life."

"He was a might slow, I reckon," Olney said coolly, "but he had the gun in his hand when I found him."

"Who shot him?"

"*Hombre* name of Soderman. But like I say, it was a fair fight."

"Like blazes!" Tack flashed. "You'll never make me believe Uncle John wore a gun! That gun was planted on him!"

"You're jumpin' to conclusions," Van Hardin said smoothly. "I saw the gun myself. There were a dozen witnesses."

"Who saw the fight?" Gentry demanded.

"They saw the gun in his hand. In his right hand," Hardin said.

Tack laughed suddenly, harshly. "That does it. Uncle John's right hand has been useless ever since Shiloh, when it was shot to pieces tryin' to get to a

41

wounded soldier. He couldn't hold a feather in those fingers, let alone a gun."

Hardin's face tightened, and Dick Olney's eyes shifted to Hardin's face.

"You'd be better off," Hardin said quietly, "to let sleepin' dogs lie. We ain't goin' to have you comin' in here stirrin' up a peaceful community."

"My uncle John was murdered," Gentry said quietly. "I mean to see his murderer punished. That ranch belongs to me. I intend to get it back."

Van Hardin smiled. "Evidently you aren't aware of what happened here," he said quietly. "Your uncle John was in a noncombatant outfit durin' the war, was he not? Well, while he was gone, the ranch he had claimed was abandoned. Soderman and I started to run cattle on that range and the land that was claimed by Bill London. No claim to the range was asserted by anyone. We made improvements, and then, durin' our temporary absence with a trail herd, John Gentry and Bill London returned and moved in. Naturally, when we returned, the case was taken to court. The court ruled the ranches belonged to Soderman and myself."

"And the cattle?" Tack asked. "What of the cattle my uncle owned?"

Hardin shrugged. "The brand had been taken over by the new owners and registered in their name. As I understand it, you left with a trail herd immediately after you came back to Texas. My claim was originally asserted during your uncle's absence. I could,"—he smiled—"lay claim to the money you got from that trail herd. Where is it?"

"Suppose you find out?" Tack replied. "I'm goin' to tell you one thing. I'm goin' to find who murdered my uncle, if it was Soderman or not. I'm also goin' to fight you in court. Now, if you'll excuse me,"—he turned his eyes to Betty who had stood, wide-eyed and silent—"I'd like to talk to Bill London."

"He can't see you," Hardin said. "He's asleep."

Gentry's eyes hardened. "You runnin' this place, too?"

"Betty London is going to work for me," Hardin replied. "We may be married later, so in a sense I'm speaking for her."

"Is that right?" Tack demanded, his eyes meeting Betty's.

Her face was miserable. "I'm afraid it is, Tack."

"You've forgotten your promise, then?" he demanded.

"Things . . . things changed, Tack," she faltered. "I . . . I can't talk about it."

"I reckon, Gentry," Olney interrupted, "it's time you rode on. There's nothin' in this neck of the woods for you. You've played out your hand here. Ride on, and you'll save yourself a lot of trouble. They're hirin' hands over on the Pecos."

"I'm stayin," Gentry said flatly.

"Remember," Olney warned, "I'm the sheriff. At the first sign of trouble, I'll come lookin' for you."

Gentry swung into the saddle. His eyes shifted to

Betty's face, and for an instant she seemed about to speak. Then he turned and rode away. He did not look back. It was not until after he was gone that he remembered Button and Blackie. To think they were in the possession of Hardin and Olney! The twin blacks he had reared and worked with, training them to do tricks, teaching them all the lore of the cow country horses and much more.

The picture was clear now. In the year in which he had been gone these men had come in, asserted their claims, taken them to carpetbag courts, and made them stick. Backing their legal claims with guns, they had taken over the country with speed and finesse. At every turn, he was blocked. Betty had turned against him. Bill London was either a prisoner in his own house or something else was wrong. Olney was sheriff, and probably they had their own judge.

He could quit. He could pull out and go on to the Pecos. It would be the easiest way. It was even what Uncle John might have wished him to do, for John Gentry was a peace-loving man. Tack Gentry was of another breed. His father had been killed fighting Comanches, and Tack had gone to war when a mere boy. Uncle John had found a place for himself in a noncombatant outfit, but Tack had fought long and well.

His ride north with the trail herd had been rough and bloody. Twice they had fought off Indians, and once they had mixed it with rustlers. In Ellsworth, a gunman named Paris had made trouble that ended with Paris dead on the floor. Tack had left town in a hurry, ridden to the new camp at Dodge, and then joined a trail herd headed for Wyoming. Indian fighting had been the order of the day, and once, rounding up a bunch of steers lost from the herd in a stampede, Tack had run into three rustlers after the same steers. Tack had downed two of them in the subsequent battle, and then shot it out with the other in a daylong rifle battle that covered a cedar- and boulder-strewn hillside. Finally, just before sundown, they met in a hand-to-hand battle with Bowie knives.

Tack remained long enough to see his old friend Major Powell, with whom he had participated in the Wagon Box fight, and then had wandered back to Kansas. On the Platte he had joined a bunch of buffalo hunters, stayed with them a couple of months, and then trailed back to Dodge.

II

Sunbonnet's Longhorn Saloon was ablaze with lights when he drifted into town that night. He stopped at the livery stable and put up his horse. He had taken a roundabout route, scouting the country, so he decided that Hardin and Olney were probably already in town. By now they would know of his call at the ranch and his meeting with Anson Childe.

He was laboring under no delusions about his future. Van Hardin would not hesitate to see him put out of the way if he attempted to regain his property.

Hardin had brains, and Olney was no fool. There were things Gentry must know before anything could be done, and the one man in town who could and would tell him was Childe.

Leaving the livery stable, he started up the street. Turning, he glanced back to see the liveryman standing in the stable door. He dropped his hand quickly, but Gentry believed he had signaled someone across the street. Yet there was no one in sight, and the row of buildings seemed blank and empty.

Only three buildings were lighted. The Longhorn, a smaller, cheaper saloon, and the old general store. There was a light upstairs over the small saloon and several lights in the annex to the Longhorn, which passed as a hotel, the only one in Sunbonnet.

Tack walked along the street, his boot heels sounding loud in the still night air. Ahead of him was a space between the buildings, and, when he drew abreast of it, he did a quick side-step off the street, flattening against the building.

He heard footsteps, hesitation, and then lightly running steps, and suddenly a man dived around the corner and grated to a stop on the gravel, staring down the alleyway between the buildings. He did not see Tack, who was flattened in the dense shadow against the building and behind a rain barrel.

The man started forward suddenly, and Tack reached out and grabbed his ankle. Caught in midstride, the fellow plunged over on his head, and then lay still. For an instant, Gentry hesitated, then struck and shielded a match with his left hand. It was the brown-hatted man he had talked to on the porch of London's ranch. His head had hit a stone, and he was out cold.

Swiftly Tack shucked the fellow's gun and emptied the shells from it, and then pushed it back in his holster. A folded paper had fallen from the unconscious man's pocket, and Tack picked it up. Then, moving fast, he went down the alley until he was in back of the small saloon. By the light from a back window, he read the note.

"This," he muttered, "may help."

Come to town quick. Trouble's brewing. We can't have anything happen now.

                                              V.H.

Van Hardin. They didn't want trouble now. Why, *now?* Folding the note, he slipped it into his pocket and flattened against the side of the saloon, studying the interior. Only two men sat in the dim interior, two men who played cards at a small table. The bartender leaned on the bar and read a newspaper. When the bartender turned his head, Tack recognized him.

Red Furness had worked for his father. He had soldiered with him. He might still be friendly. Tack lifted his knuckles and tapped lightly on the window.

At the second tap, Red looked up. Tack lighted a match and moved it past the window. Neither of the card players seemed to have noticed. Red straightened, folded his paper, and then, picking up a cup, walked back toward the window. When he got there, he dipped the cup into the water bucket with one hand and with the other lifted the window a few inches.

"This is Tack Gentry. Where does Childe hang out?"

Red's whisper was low. "Got him an office and sleepin' room upstairs. There's a back stairway. You watch yourself."

Tack stepped away from his window and made his way to the stairway he had already glimpsed. It might be a trap, but he believed Red was loyal. Also, he was not sure the word was out to kill him. They probably merely wanted him out of the way and hoped he could be warned to move on. The position of the Hardin group seemed secure enough.

Reaching the top of the stairs, he walked along the narrow catwalk to the door. He tapped softly. After an instant, there was a voice. "What do you want?"

"This is Tack Gentry. You talked to me in the saloon." The door opened to darkness, and he stepped in. When it closed, he felt a pistol barrel against his spine.

"Hold still," Childe warned.

Behind him a match struck, and then a candle was lighted. The light still glowed in the other room, seen only by the crack under the door. Childe grinned at him. "Got to be careful," he said. "They have tried twice to dry-gulch me. I put flowers on their graves every Monday." He smiled. "And keep an extra one dug. Ever since I had that new grave dug, I've been left alone. Somehow it seems to have a very sobering influence on the local roughs." He sat down. "I tire quicker than I once did. So you're Gentry. Betty London told me about you. She thought you were dead. There was a rumor that you'd been killed by the Indians in Wyoming."

"No, I came out all right. What I want to know, rememberin' you said you were a lawyer, is what kind of a claim do they have on my ranch?"

"A good one, unfortunately. While you and your uncle were gone, and most of the other men in the locality, several of these men came in and began to brand cattle. After branding a good many, they left. They returned and began working around, about the time you left, and then they ordered your uncle off. He wouldn't go, and they took the case to court. There were no lawyers here then, and your uncle tried to handle it himself. The judge was their man, and suddenly a half dozen witnesses appeared and were sworn in. They testified that the land had been taken and held by Soderman, Olney, and Hardin. They claimed their brands on the cattle asserted their claim to the land, to the home ranches of both London and Gentry. The free range was something else, but with the two big ranches in their hands and the bulk of the free range lying beyond their holdings, they were in a position to freeze out the smaller ranchers. They established a squatter's right to each of the big ranches."

"Can they do that?" Tack demanded. "It doesn't seem fair."

"The usual thing is to allow no claim unless they have occupied the land for twenty years without hindrance, but with a carpetbag court they do about as they please. Judge Weaver is completely in Van Hardin's hands, and your uncle John was on the losing side in this war."

"How did Uncle John get killed?" Tack asked.

Childe shrugged. "They said he called Soderman a liar and Soderman went for his gun. Your uncle had a gun on him when they found him. It was probably a cold-blooded killing because Gentry planned on a trip to Austin and was going to appeal the case."

"Have you seen Bill London lately?"

"Only once since the accident."

"Accident?"

"Yes, London was headed for home, dozing along in the buckboard as he always did, when his team ran away with him. The buckboard was overturned and London's back was injured. He can't ride any more and can't sit up very long at a time."

"Was it really an accident?" Tack wanted to know.

Childe shrugged. "I doubt it. We couldn't prove a thing. One of the horses had a bad cut on the hip. It looked as if someone with a steel-tipped bullwhip had hit the animal from beside the road."

"Thorough," Tack said. "They don't miss a bet."

Childe nodded. Leaning back in his chair, he put his feet on the desk. He studied Tack Gentry thought-

50

fully. "You know, you'll be next. They won't stand for you messing around. I think you already have them worried."

Tack explained about the man following him, and then handed the note to Childe. The lawyer's eyes narrowed. "*Hmm*, sounds like they had some reason to soft-pedal the whole thing for a while. Maybe it's an idea for us. Maybe somebody is coming down here to look around, or maybe somebody has grown suspicious."

Tack looked at Childe thoughtfully. "What's your position in all this?"

The tall man shrugged, and then laughed lightly. "I've no stake in it, Gentry. I didn't know London or your uncle John, either. But I heard rumors, and I didn't like the attitude of the local bosses, Hardin and Olney. I'm just a burr under the saddle with which they ride this community, no more. It amuses me to needle them, and they are afraid of me."

"Got any clients?"

"Clients?" Anson Childe chuckled. "Not a one. Not likely to have any, either. In a country so throttled by one man as this is, there isn't any litigation. Nobody can win against him, and they are too busy hating Hardin to want to have trouble with each other."

"Well, then," Tack said, "you've got a client now. Go down to Austin. Demand an investigation. Lay the facts on the table for them. Maybe you can't do any good, but at least you can stir up a lot of trouble. The main thing will be to get people talking. They evidently want quiet, so we'll give them noise. Find out all you can. Get some detectives started on Hardin's trail. Find out who they are, who they were, and where they came from."

Childe sat up. "I'd like it," he said ruefully, "but I don't have that kind of money." He gestured at the room. "I'm behind on my rent here. Red owns the building, so he lets me stay."

Tack grinned and unbuttoned his shirt, drawing out a money belt. "I sold some cattle up north." He counted out $1,000. "Take that. Spend all or any part of it, but create a smell down there. Tell everybody about the situation here."

Childe got up, his face flushed with enthusiasm. "Man, nothing could please me more. I'll make it hot for them. I'll. . . ." He went into a fit of coughing, and Tack watched him gravely. Finally Childe straightened. "You're putting your trust in a sick man, Gentry."

"I'm putting my trust in a fighter," Tack said dryly. "You'll do." He hesitated briefly. "Also, check the title on this land."

They shook hands silently, and Tack went to the door. Softly he opened it and stepped out into the cool night. Well, for better or worse the battle was opened now for the next step. He came down off the wooden stairs, and then walked to the street. There was no one it sight. Tack Gentry crossed the street and pushed through the swinging doors of the Longhorn.

The saloon and dance hall was crowded. A few

familiar faces, but they were sullen faces, lined and hard. The faces of bitter men, defeated, but not whipped. The others were new faces, the hard, tough faces of gun hands, the weather-beaten cowpunchers who had come in to take the new jobs. He pushed his way to the bar.

There were three bartenders now, and it wasn't until he ordered that the squat, fat man glanced down the bar and saw him. His jaw hardened and he spoke to the bartender who was getting a bottle to pour Gentry's rye.

The bartender, a lean, sallow-faced man, strolled back to him. "We're not servin' you," he said. "I got my orders."

Tack reached across the bar, his hand shooting out so fast the bartender had no chance to withdraw. Catching the man by his stiff collar, two fingers inside the collar and their knuckles jammed hard into the man's Adam's apple, he jerked him to the bar.

"Pour!" he said.

The man tried to speak, but Tack gripped harder and shoved back on the knuckles. Weakly, desperately, his face turning blue, the man poured. He slopped out twice what he got in the glass, but he poured. Then Tack shoved hard and the man brought up violently against the backbar.

Tack lifted his glass with his left hand, his eyes sweeping the crowd, all of whom had drawn back slightly. "To honest ranchers!" he said loudly and clearly and downed his drink.

A big, hard-faced man shoved through the crowd. "Maybe you're meanin' some of us ain't honest?" he suggested.

"That's right!" Tack Gentry let his voice ring out in the room, and he heard the *rattle* of chips cease, and the shuffling of feet died away. The crowd was listening. "That's exactly right! There were honest men here, but they were murdered or crippled. My uncle John Gentry was murdered. They tried to make it look like a fair and square killin' . . . they stuck a gun in his hand!"

"That's right!" A man broke in. "He had a gun! I seen it!"

Tack's eyes shifted. "What hand was it in?"

"His right hand!" the man stated positively, belligerently. "I seen it!"

"Thank you, pardner," Tack said politely. "The gun was in John Gentry's right hand . . . and John Gentry's right hand had been paralyzed ever since Shiloh!"

"Huh?" The man who had seen the gun stepped back, his face whitening a little.

Somebody back in the crowd shouted out: "That's right! You're durn' tootin' that's right! Never could use a rope 'count of it!"

Tack looked around at the crowd, and his eyes halted on the big man. He was going to break the power of Hardin, Olney, and Soderman, and he was going to start right here.

"There's goin' to be an investigation," he said

loudly, "and it'll begin down in Austin. Any of you fellers bought property from Hardin, or Olney better get your money back."

"You're talkin' a lot!" The big man thrust toward him, his wide, heavy shoulders looking broad enough for two men. "You said some of us were thieves!"

"Thieves and murderers," Tack added. "If you're one of the worms that crawl in Hardin's tracks, that goes for you!"

The big man lunged.

"Get him, Starr!" somebody shouted loudly.

Tack Gentry suddenly felt a fierce surge of pure animal joy. He stepped back, and then stepped in suddenly, and his right swung, low and hard. It caught Starr as he was coming in, caught him in the pit of the stomach. He grunted and stopped dead in his tracks, but Tack set himself and swung wickedly with both hands. His left smashed into Starr's mouth, and his right split a cut over his cheek bone. Starr staggered and fell back into the crowd. He came out of the crowd, shook his head, and charged like a bull.

Tack weaved inside of the swinging fists and impaled the bigger man on a straight, hard left hand. Then he crossed a wicked right to the cut cheek, and gore cascaded down the man's face. Tack stepped in, smashing both hands to the man's body, and then, as Starr stabbed a thumb at his eye, Tack jerked his head aside and butted Starr in the face.

His nose broken, his cheek laid open to the bone,

Starr staggered back, and Tack Gentry walked in, swinging with both hands. This was the beginning. This man worked for Hardin and he was going to be an example. When he left this room, Starr's face was going to be a sample of the crashing of Van Hardin's power. With left and right he cut and slashed at the big man's face, and Starr, overwhelmed by the attack, helpless after that first wicked body blow, crumpled under those smashing fists. He hit the floor suddenly and lay there, moaning softly.

A man shoved through the crowd, and then stopped. It was Van Hardin. He looked down at the man on the floor, then his eyes, dark with hate, lifted to meet Tack Gentry's eyes.

"Lookin' for trouble, are you?" he said.

"Only catchin' up with some that started while I was gone, Van," Tack said. He felt good. He was on the balls of his feet and ready. He had liked the jarring of blows, liked the feeling of combat. He was ready. "You should have made sure I was dead, Hardin, before you tried to steal property from a kindly old man."

"Nothing was stolen," Van Hardin said evenly, calmly. "We took only what was ours, and in a strictly legal manner."

"There will be an investigation," Gentry replied bluntly, "from Austin. Then we'll thrash the whole thing out."

Hardin's eyes sharpened and he was suddenly wary. "An investigation? What makes you think so?"

Tack was aware that Hardin was worried. "Because I'm startin' it. I'm askin' for it, and I'll get it. There was a lot you didn't know about that land you stole, Hardin. You were like most crooks. You could only see your side of the question and it looked very simple and easy, but there's always the thing you overlook, and *you* overlooked somethin'."

The doors swung wide and Olney pushed into the room. He stopped, glancing from Hardin to Gentry. "What goes on here?" he demanded.

"Gentry is accusin' us of bein' thieves," Hardin said carelessly.

Olney turned and faced Tack. "He's in no position to accuse anybody of anything," he said. "I'm arrestin' him for murder!"

There was a stir in the room, and Tack Gentry felt the sudden sickness of fear. "Murder? Are you crazy?" he demanded.

"I'm not, but you may be," the sheriff said. "I've just come from the office of Anson Childe. He's been murdered. You were his last visitor. You were observed sneaking into his place by the back stairs. You were observed sneaking out of it. I'm arresting you for murder."

The room was suddenly still, and Tack Gentry felt the rise of hostility toward him. Many men had admired the courage of Anson Childe; many men had been helped by him. Frightened themselves, they had enjoyed his flouting of Hardin and Olney. Now he was dead, murdered.

"Childe was my friend," Tack protested. "He was goin' to Austin for me."

Hardin laughed sarcastically. "You mean he knew you had no case and refused to go, and in a fit of rage you killed him. You shot him."

"You'll have to come with me," Olney said grimly. "You'll get a fair trial."

Silently Tack looked at him. Swiftly thoughts raced through his mind. There was no chance for escape. The crowd was too thick, and he had no idea if there was a horse out front, although there no doubt was, but his own horse was in the livery stable. Olney relieved him of his gun belt and they started toward the door. Starr, leaning against the doorpost, his face raw as chewed beef, glared at him evilly.

"I'll be seein' you," he said softly. "Soon."

Soderman and Hardin had fallen in around him, and behind them were two of Hardin's roughs.

The jail was small, just four cells and an outer office. The door of one of the cells was opened and he was shoved inside. Hardin grinned at him. "This should settle the matter for Austin," he said. "Childe had friends down there."

Anson Childe murdered! Tack Gentry, numbed by the blow, stared at the stone wall. He had counted on Childe, counted on his stirring up an investigation. Once an investigation was started, he possessed two aces in the hole he could use to defeat Hardin in court, but it demanded a court not controlled by Hardin. With Childe's death he had no friends on the outside. Betty had barely spoken to him when they met, and, if she was going to work for Hardin in his dance hall, she must have changed much. Bill London was a cripple and unable to get around. Red Furness, for all his friendship, wouldn't come out in the open. Tack had no illusions about the murder. By the time the case came to trial, they would have found ample evidence. They had his guns and they could fire two or three shots from them, whatever had been used on Childe. It would be a simple thing to frame him. Hardin would have no trouble in finding witnesses.

He was standing, staring out the small window, its lower sill just on the level of his eyes, when he heard a distant rumble of thunder and a jagged streak of lightning brightened the sky, followed by more thunder. The rains came slowly, softly, and then in steadily increasing volume. The jail was still and empty. Sounds of music and occasional shouts sounded from the Longhorn, then the roar of rain drowned them out. He threw himself down on the cot in the corner of the room and, lulled by the falling rain, was soon asleep.

A long time later, he awakened. The rain was still falling, but above it was another sound. Listening, he suddenly realized what it was. The dry wash behind the town was running, probably bank full. Lying there in the darkness, he became aware of still another sound, of the nearer rushing of water. Lifting his head, he listened. Then he got to his feet and crossed the small cell.

Water was running under the corner of the jail. There had been a good deal of rain lately, and he had noted that the barrel at the corner of the jail had been full. It was overflowing, and the water had evidently washed under the corner of the building.

He walked back and sat down on the bed, and, as he listened to the water, an idea came to him suddenly. Tack got up and went to the corner of the cell. Striking a match, he studied the wall and floor. Both were damp. He stamped on the stone flags of the floor, but they were solid. He kicked at the wall. It was also solid.

How thick were those walls? Judging by what he remembered of the door, the walls were all of eight inches thick, but how about the floor? Kneeling on the floor, he struck another match, studying the mortar around the corner flagstone.

Then he felt in his pockets. There was nothing there he could use to dig that mortar. His pocket knife, his Bowie knife, his keys—all were gone. Suddenly he had an inspiration. Slipping off his wide leather belt, he began to dig at the mortar with the edge of his heavy brass belt buckle.

The mortar was damp, but he worked steadily. His hands slipped on the sweaty buckle and he skinned his fingers and knuckles on the rough stone floor, yet he persevered, scraping, scratching, digging out tiny fragments of mortar. From time to time he straightened up and stamped on the stone. It was solid as Gibraltar.

Five hours he scraped and scratched, digging until his belt buckle was no longer of use. He had scraped out almost two inches of mortar. Sweeping up the scattered grains of mortar, and digging some of the mud off his boots, he filled in the cracks as best he could. Then he walked to his bunk and sprawled out and was instantly asleep.

III

Early in the morning, he heard someone stirring around outside. Then Olney walked back to his cell and looked in at him. Starr followed in a few minutes, carrying a plate of food and a pot of coffee. His face was badly bruised and swollen, and his eyes were hot with hate. He put the food down, and then walked away. Olney loitered.

"Gentry," he said suddenly, "I hate to see a good hand in this spot."

Tack looked up. "I'll bet you do," he said sarcastically.

"No use takin' that attitude," Olney protested, "after all, you made trouble for us. Why couldn't you leave well enough alone? You were in the clear, you had a few dollars apparently, and you could do all right. Hardin took possession of those ranches legally. He can hold 'em, too."

"We'll see."

61

"No, I mean it. He can. Why don't you drop the whole thing?"

"Drop it?" Tack laughed. "How can I drop it? I'm in jail for murder now, and you know as well as I do I never killed Anson Childe. This trial will smoke the whole story out of its hole. I mean to see that it does."

Olney winced, and Tack could see he had touched a tender spot. That was what they were afraid of. They had him now, but they didn't want him. They wanted nothing so much as to be completely rid of him.

"Only make trouble for folks," Olney protested. "You won't get nowhere. You can bet that, if you go to trial, we'll have all the evidence we need."

"Sure. I know I'll be framed."

"What can you expect?" Olney shrugged. "You're askin' for it. Why don't you play smart? If you'd leave the country, we could sort of arrange maybe to turn you loose."

Tack looked up at him. "You mean that?" *Like blazes,* he told himself. *I can see you turnin' me loose! And when I walked out, you'd have somebody there to smoke me down, shot escaping jail. Yeah, I know.* "If I thought you'd let me go. . . ." He hesitated, angling to get Olney's reaction.

The sheriff put his head close to the bars. "You know me, Tack," he whispered. "I don't want to see you stick your head in a noose. Sure, you spoke out of turn, and you tried to scare up trouble for us, but if you'd leave, I think I could arrange it."

"Just give me the chance," Tack assured him

"Once I get out of here, I'll really start movin'." *And that's no lie*, he added to himself.

Olney went away, and the morning dragged slowly. They would let him go. He was praying now they would wait until the next day. Yet even if they did permit him to escape, even if they did not have him shot as he was leaving, what could he do? Childe, his best means of assistance, was dead. At every turn he was stopped. They had the law, and they had the guns.

His talk the night before would have implanted doubts. His whipping of Starr would have pleased many, and some of them would realize that his arrest for the murder of Childe was a frame. Yet none of these people would do anything about it without leadership. None of them wanted his own neck in a noose.

Olney dropped in later and leaned close to the bars. "I'll have something arranged by tomorrow," he said.

Tack lay back on the bunk and fell asleep. All day the rain had continued without interruption except for a few minutes at a time. The hills would be soggy now, the trails bad. He could hear the wash running strongly, running like a river not thirty yards behind the jail.

Darkness fell, and he ate again, and then returned to his bunk. With a good lawyer and a fair judge he could beat them in court. He had an ace in the hole that would help, and another that might do the job.

He waited until the jail was silent and he could hear the usual sounds from the Longhorn. Then he got up

63

and walked over to the corner. All day water had been running under the corner of the jail and must have excavated a fair-size hole by now. Tack knelt down and took from his pocket the fork he had secreted after his meal.

Olney, preoccupied with plans to allow Tack Gentry to escape and sure that Tack was accepting the plan had paid little attention to the returned plate.

On his knees, Tack dug out the loosely filled in dust and dirt, and then began digging frantically at the hole. He worked steadily for an hour, and then crossed to the bucket for a drink of water and to stretch, and then he returned to work.

Another hour passed. He got up and stamped on the stone. It seemed to sink under his feet. He bent his knees and jumped, coming down hard on his heels. The stone gave way so suddenly he almost went through. He caught himself, withdrew his feet from the hole, and bent over, striking a match. It was no more than six inches to the surface of the water, and even a glance told him it must be much deeper than he had believed.

He took another look, waited an instant, and then lowered his feet into the water. The current jerked at them, and then he lowered his body through the hole and let go. Instantly he was jerked away and literally thrown downstream. He caught a quick glimpse of a light from a window, and then he was whirling over and over. He grabbed frantically, hoping to get his hands on something, but they clutched only empty air. Frantically he fought toward where there must be a bank, realizing he was in a roaring stream all of six feet deep. He struck nothing and was thrown, almost hurtled, downstream with what seemed to be over-whelming speed. Something black loomed near him, and at the same instant the water caught at him, rushing with even greater power. He grabbed again at the blob of blackness, and his hand caught a root.

Yet it was nothing secure, merely a huge cotton-wood log rushing downstream. Working his way along it, he managed to get a leg over and crawled atop it. Fortunately the log did not roll over.

Lying there in the blackness, he realized what must have happened. Behind the row of buildings that fronted on the street, of which the jail was one, was a shallow, sandy ditch. At one end of it the bluff reared up. The dry wash skirted one side of the triangle formed by the bluff, and the ditch formed the other. Water flowing off the bluff and off the roofs of the buildings and from the street of the town and the rise beyond it had flooded into the ditch, washing it deeper. Yet now he knew he was in the current of the wash itself, now running bank full, a raging torrent.

A brief flash of lightning revealed the stream down which he was shooting like a chip in a millrace. Below, he knew, was Cathedral Gorge, a narrow boulder-strewn gash in the mountain down which this wash would thunder like an express train. Tack had seen logs go down it, smashing into boulders, hurled against the rocky walls, and then shooting at last out into the open flat below the gorge. And he knew instantly that no living thing could hope to ride a charging log through the black, roaring depths of the gorge and come out anything but a mangled, lifeless pulp.

The log he was bestriding hit a wave, and water drenched him. Then the log whirled dizzily around a bend in the wash. Before him and around another bend he could hear the roar of the gorge. The log swung, and then the driving roots ripped into a heap of débris at the bend of the wash, and the log swung wickedly across the current. Scrambling like a madman, Tack fought his way toward the roots, and then, even as the log ripped loose, he hurled himself at the heap of débris.

He landed in a heap of broken boughs, and felt something gouge him, and then, scrambling, he made the rocks and clambered up into their shelter, lying there on a flat rock, gasping for breath.

A long time later he got up. Something was wrong with his right leg. It felt numb and sore. He crawled over the rocks and stumbled over the muddy earth toward the partial shelter of a clump of trees.

He needed shelter, and he needed a gun. Tack Gentry knew that now that he was free they would scour the country for him. They might believe him dead, but they would want to be certain. What he needed now was shelter, rest, and food. He needed to examine himself to see how badly he was injured, yet where could he turn?

Betty? She was too far away and he had no horse. Red Furness? Possibly, but how much the man would or could help he did not know. Yet thinking of Red made him think of Childe. There was a place for him. If he could only get to Childe's quarters over the saloon!

Luckily he had landed on the same side of the wash as the town. He was stiff and sore, and his leg was paining him grievously. Yet there was no time to be lost. What the hour was he had no idea, but he knew his progress would be slow, and he must be careful. The rain was pounding down, but he was so wet now that it made no difference.

How long it took him he never knew. He could have been no more than a mile from town, perhaps less, and he walked, crawled, and pulled himself to the edge of town, and then behind the buildings until he reached the dark back stairway to Anson Childe's room. Step by step he crawled up. Fortunately the door was unlocked.

Once inside, he stood there in the darkness, listening. There was no sound. This room was windowless but for one very small and tightly curtained window at the top of the wall. Tack felt for the candle, found it, and fumbled for a match. When he had the candle alight, he started pulling off his clothes.

Naked, he dried himself with a towel, avoiding the injured leg. Then he found a bottle and poured himself a drink. He tossed it off, and then sat down on the edge of the bed and looked at his leg.

It almost made him sick to look at it. Hurled against a root or something in the dark, he had torn a great, mangled wound in the calf of his leg. No artery appeared to have been injured, but in places his shin bone was visible through the ripped flesh. The wound in the calf was deeper. Cleansing it as best he could, he found a white shirt belonging to Childe and bandaged his leg.

Exhausted, he fell asleep—when, he never recalled. Only hours later he awakened suddenly to find sunlight streaming through the door into the front room. His leg was stiff and sore, and, when he moved, it throbbed with pain. Using a cane he found hanging in the room, he pulled himself up and staggered to the door.

The curtains in the front room were up and sunlight streamed in. The rain seemed to be gone. From where he stood he could see into the street, and almost the first person he saw was Van Hardin. He was standing in front of the Longhorn talking to Soderman and the mustached man Tack had first seen at his own ranch.

The sight reminded him, and Tack hunted around for a gun. He found a pair of beautifully matched Colts, silver-plated and ivory-handled. He strapped them on with their ornate belt and holsters. Then, standing in a corner, he found a riot gun and a Henry rifle. He checked the loads in all the guns, found several boxes of ammunition for each of them, and emptied a box of .45s into the pockets of a pair of Childe's pants he pulled on. Then he put a double handful of shotgun shells into the pockets of a leather jacket he found. He sat down then, for he was weak and trembling.

IV

His time was short. Sooner or later someone would come to this room. Either someone would think of it, or someone would come to claim the room for himself. Red Furness had no idea he was there, so would probably not hesitate to let anyone come up.

He locked the door, and then dug around and found a stale loaf of bread and some cheese. Then he lay down to rest. His leg was throbbing with pain, and he knew it needed care, and badly.

When he awakened, he studied the street from a vantage point well inside the room and to one side of the window. Several knots of men were standing around talking, more men than should have been in town at that hour. He recognized one or two of them as being old-timers around. Twice he saw Olney ride by, and the sheriff was carrying a riot gun.

Starr and the mustached man were loafing in front of the Longhorn, and two other men Tack recognized as coming from the old London Ranch were there.

He ate some more bread and cheese. He was just finishing his sandwich when a buckboard turned into the street, and his heart jumped when he saw Betty London was driving. Beside her in the seat was her father, Bill, worn and old, his hair white now, but he was wearing a gun!

Something was stirring down below. It began to look as if the lid was about to blow off. Yet Tack had no idea of his own status. He was an escaped prisoner and as such could be shot on sight legally by Olney or Starr, who seemed to be a deputy. From the wary attitude of the Van Hardin men he knew that they were disturbed by their lack of knowledge of him.

Yet the day passed without incident, and finally he returned to the bunk and lay down after checking his guns once more. The time for the payoff was near, he knew. It could come at any moment. He was lying there, thinking about that and looking up at the rough plank ceiling when he heard steps on the stairs.

He arose so suddenly that a twinge of pain shot through the weight that had become his leg. The steps were on the front stairs, not the back. A quick glance from the window told him it was Betty London. What did she want here?

Her hand fell on the knob and it turned. He eased off the bed and turned the key in the lock. She hesitated just an instant, and then stepped in. When their eyes met, hers went wide, and her face went white to the lips.

"You!" she gasped. "Oh, Tack! What have you been doing? Where have you been?"

She started toward him, but he backed up and sat down on the bed. "Wait. Do they know I'm up here?" he demanded harshly.

"No, Tack. I came up to see if some papers were here, some papers I gave to Anson Childe before he was . . . murdered."

"You think I did that?" he demanded.

"No, of course not." Her eyes held a question. "Tack, what's the matter? Don't you like me any more?"

"Don't I like you?" His lips twisted with bitterness. "Lady, you've got a nerve to ask that. I come back and find my girl about to go dancin' in a cheap saloon dance hall, and. . . ."

"I needed money, Tack," Betty said quietly. "Dad needed care. We didn't have any money. Everything we had was lost when we lost the ranch. Hardin offered me the job. He said he wouldn't let anybody molest me."

"What about him?"

"I could take care of him." She looked at him, puzzled. "Tack, what's the matter? Why are you sitting down? Are you hurt?"

"My leg." He shook his head as she started forward. "Don't bother about it. There's no time. What are they saying down there? What's all the crowd in town? Give it to me, quick."

"Some of them think you were drowned in escaping from jail. I don't think Van Hardin thinks that, nor Olney. They seem very disturbed. The crowd is in town for Childe's funeral and because some of them think you were murdered once Olney got you in jail. Some of our old friends."

"Betty!" The call came from the street below. It was Van Hardin's voice.

"Don't answer." Tack Gentry got up. His dark green eyes were hard. "I want him to come up."

Betty waited, her eyes wide, listening. Footsteps sounded on the stairway, and then the door shoved open. "Bet. . . ." Van Hardin's voice died out and he stood there, one hand on the doorknob, staring at Tack.

"Howdy, Hardin," Tack said, "I was hopin' you'd come."

Van Hardin said nothing. His powerful shoulders filled the open door, his eyes were set, and the shock was fading from them now.

"Got a few things to tell you, Hardin," Tack continued gently. "Before you go out of this feet first, I want you to know what a sucker you've been."

"A sucker I've been?" Hardin laughed. "What chance have you got? The street down there is full of my men. You've friends there, too, but they lack leadership. They don't know what to do. My men have their orders. And then I won't have any trouble with you, Gentry. Your old friends around here told me all about you. Soft, like that uncle of yours."

"Ever hear of Black Jack Paris, Hardin?"

"The gunman? Of course, but what's he got to do with you?"

"Nothin', now. He did once, up in Ellsworth, Kansas. They dug a bed for him next mornin', Hardin. He was too slow. You said I was soft? Well, maybe I was once. Maybe in spots I still am, but you see, since the folks around here have seen me, I've been over the cattle trails, been doin' some Injun fightin', and rustler killin'. It makes a sight of change in a man, Hardin. But that ain't what I wanted you to know. I wanted you to know what a fool you were, tryin' to steal this ranch. You see, the land in our home ranch wasn't like the rest of this land, Hardin."

"What do you mean?" Hardin demanded suspiciously.

"Why, you're the smart boy," Tack drawled easily. "You should have checked before takin' so much for granted. You see, the Gentry Ranch was a land grant. My grandmother, she was a Basque, see? The land came to us through her family, and the will she left was that it would belong to us as long as any of us lived, that it couldn't be sold or traded, and in case we all died, it was to go to the state of Texas."

Van Hardin stared. "What?" he gasped. "What kind of fool deal is this you're givin' me?"

"Fool deal is right." Tack said quietly. "You see, the state of Texas knows no Gentry would sell or trade, knowin' we couldn't, so if somebody else showed up with the land, they were bound to ask a sight of questions. Sooner or later they'd have got around to askin' you how come."

Hardin seemed stunned. From the street below, there was a sound of horses' hoofs.

Then a voice said from Tack's left: "You better get

73

out, Van. There's talkin' to be done in the street. want Tack Gentry."

Tack's head jerked around. It was Soderman. The short, squinty-eyed man was staring at him, gun in hand. He heard Hardin turn and bolt out of the room saw resolution in Soderman's eyes. Hurling himsel toward the wall, Gentry's hand flashed for his pistol

A gun blasted in the room with a roar like a cannon and Gentry felt the angry whip of the bullet, and ther he fired twice, low down. Soderman fell back agains the doorjamb, both hands grabbing at his stomach just below his belt buckle. "You shot me!" he gasped round eyed. "You shot . . . me!"

"Like you did my uncle," Tack said coolly. "Only you had better than an even break, and he had no break at all."

Gentry could feel blood from the opened woun trickling down his leg. He glanced at Betty. "I've go to get down there," he said. "He's a slick talker."

Van Hardin was standing down in the street. Besid him was Olney and nearby was Starr. Other men, half dozen of them, loitered nearby.

Slowly Tack Gentry began stumping down the stair All eyes looked up. Red Furness saw him and spok out: "Tack, these three men are Rangers come dow from Austin to make some inquiries."

Hardin pointed at Gentry. "He's wanted for mur dering Anson Childe! Also for jail breaking, an unless I'm much mistaken he has killed another ma up there in Childe's office!"

74

The Rangers looked at him curiously, and then one of them glanced at Hardin. "You-all the *hombre* what lays claim to the Gentry place?"

Hardin swallowed quickly, and then his eyes shifted. "No, that was Soderman. The man who was upstairs."

Hardin looked at Tack Gentry. With the Rangers here he knew his game was played out. He smiled suddenly. "You've nothin' on me at all, gents," he said coolly. "Soderman killed John Gentry and laid claim to his ranch. I don't know nothin' about it."

"You engineered it!" Bill London burst out. "Same as you did the stealin' of my ranch!"

"You've no proof," Hardin sneered. "Not a particle. My name is on no papers, and you have no evidence."

Coolly he strode across to his black horse and swung into the saddle. He was smiling gently, but there was sneering triumph behind the smile. "You've nothin' on me, not a thing."

"Don't let him him get away!" Bill London shouted. "He's the wust one of the whole kit and kaboodle of 'em!"

"But he's right," the Ranger protested. "In all the papers we've found, there's not a single item to tie him up. If he's in it, he's been almighty smart."

"Then arrest him for horse stealin'," Tack Gentry said. "That's my black horse he's on."

Hardin's face went cold, and then he smiled. "Why, that's crazy! That's foolish," he said. "This is my horse. I reared him from a colt. Anybody could be

75

mistaken, 'cause one black horse is like another. My brand's on him, and you can all see it's an old brand."

Tack Gentry stepped out in front of the black horse. "Button!" he said sharply. "Button!"

At the familiar voice, the black horse's head jerked up.

"Button!" Tack called. "Hut! Hut!"

As the name and the sharp command rolled out, Button reacted like an explosion of dynamite. He jumped straight up in the air and came down hard. Then he sunfished wildly, and Van Hardin hit the dirt in a heap.

"Button!" Tack commanded. "Go get Blackie!"

Instantly the horse wheeled and trotted to the hitching rail where Blackie stood ground-hitched as Olney had left him. Button caught the reins in his teeth and led the other black horse back.

The Ranger grinned. "Reckon, mister," he said, "you done proved your case. The man's a horse thief."

Hardin climbed to his feet, his face dark with fury. "You think you'll get away with that?" His hand flashed for his gun.

Tack Gentry had been watching him, and now his own hand moved down and then up. The two guns barked as one. A chip flew from the stair post beside Tack, but Van Hardin turned slowly and went to his knees in the dust.

At almost the same instant, a sharp voice rang out. "Olney! Starr!"

Olney's face went white and he wheeled, hand flashing for his gun. "Anson Childe," he gasped.

Childe stood on the platform in front of his room and fired once, twice, three times. Sheriff Olney went down, coughing and muttering. Starr backed through the swinging doors of the saloon and sat down hard in the sawdust.

Tack stared at him. "What the . . . ?"

The tall young lawyer came down the steps. "Fooled them, didn't I? They tried to get me once too often. I got their man with a shotgun in the face. Then I changed clothes with him and lit out for Austin. I came in with the Rangers, and then left them on the edge of town. They told me they'd let us have it our way unless they were needed."

"Saves the state of Texas a sight of money," one of the Rangers drawled. "Anyway, we been checkin' on this here Hardin. On Olney, too. That's why they wanted to keep things quiet around here. They knowed we was checkin' on 'em."

The Rangers moved in and with the help of a few of the townspeople rounded up Hardin's other followers.

Tack grinned at the lawyer. "Lived up to your name, pardner," he said. "You sure did! All your sheep in the fold, now."

"What do you mean? Lived up to my name?" Anson Childe looked around.

Gentry grinned. "And a little Childe shall lead hem," he said.

Dutchman's Flat

The dust of Dutchman's Flat had settled in a gray film upon their faces, and Neill could see the streaks made by the sweat on their cheeks and brows and knew his own must be the same. No man of them was smiling and they rode with their rifles in their hands, six grim and purposeful men upon the trail of a single rider.

They were men shaped and tempered to the harsh ways of a harsh land, strong in their sense of justice, ruthless in their demand for punishment, relentless in pursuit. From the desert they had carved their homes, and from the desert they drew their courage and their code, and the desert knows no mercy.

"Where's he headin', you reckon?"

"Home, mostly likely. He'll need grub an' a rifle. He's been livin' on the old Sorenson place."

Kimmel spat. "He's welcome to it. That place starved out four men I know of." He stared at the hoof tracks ahead. "He's got a good horse."

"Big buckskin. Reckon we'll catch him, Hardin?"

"Sure. Not this side of his place, though. There ain't no short cuts we can take to head him off, and he's pointin' for home straight as a horse can travel."

"Ain't tryin' to cover his trail none."

"No use tryin'." Hardin squinted his eyes against the glare of the sun. "He knows we figure he'll head for his ranch."

"He's no tenderfoot." Kesney expressed the thought

79

that had been dawning upon them all in the last two hours. "He knows how to save a horse, an' he knows a trail."

They rode on in near silence. Hardin scratched his unshaven jaw. The dust lifted from the hoofs of the horses as they weaved their way through the catclaw and mesquite. It was a parched and sun-baked land, with only dancing heat waves and the blue distance of the mountains to draw them on. The trail they followed led straight as a man could ride across the country. Only at draws or nests of rocks did it swerve, where they noticed the rider always gave his horse the best of it.

No rider of the desert must see a man to know him for it is enough to follow his trail. In these things are the ways of a man made plain, his kindness or cruelty, his ignorance or cunning, his strength and his weakness. There are indications that cannot escape a man who has followed trails, and in the two hours since they had ridden out of Freedom the six had already learned much of the man they followed. And they would learn more.

"What started it?"

The words sounded empty and alone in the vast stillness of the basin.

Hardin turned his head slightly so the words could drift back. It was the manner of a man who rides much in the wind or rain. He shifted the rifle to his left hand and wiped his sweaty right palm on his coarse pants leg.

"Some loose talk. He was in the Bon Ton buyin' grub an' such. Johnny said somethin' at which he took offense, an' they had some words. Johnny was wearin' a gun, but this Lock wasn't, so he gets him a gun an' goes over to the Longhorn. He pushes open the door an' shoots Johnny twice through the body. In the back." Hardin spat. "He fired a third shot, but that missed Johnny and busted a bottle of whiskey."

There was a moment's silence while they digested this, and then Neill looked up.

"We lynchin' him for the killin' or bustin' the whiskey?"

It was a good question, but drew no reply. The dignity of the five other riders was not to be touched by humor. They were riders on a mission. Neill let his eyes drift over the dusty copper of the desert. He had no liking for the idea of lynching any man, and he did not know the squatter from the Sorenson place. Living there should be punishment enough for any man. Besides. . . ."Who saw the shooting?" he asked.

"Nobody seen it, actually. Only he never gave Johnny a fair shake. Sam was behind the bar, but he was down to the other end and it happened too fast."

"What's his name? Somebody call him Lock?" Neill asked. There was something incongruous in lynching a man whose name you did not know. He shifted in the saddle, squinting his eyes toward the distant lakes dancing in the mirage of heat waves.

"What's it matter? Lock, his name is. Chat Lock."

"Funny name."

The comment drew no response. The dust was thicker now and Neill pulled his bandanna over his nose and mouth. His eyes were drawn back to the distant blue of the lakes. They were enticingly cool and beautiful, lying across the way ahead and in the basin off to the right. This was the mirage that lured many a man from his trail to pursue the always retreating shoreline of the lake. It looked like water, it really did.

Maybe there was water in the heat waves. Maybe if a man knew how, he could extract it and drink. The thought drew his hand to his canteen, but he took it away without drinking. The *sloshing* water in the canteen was no longer enticing, for it was warm, brackish, and unsatisfying.

"You know him, Kimmel?" Kesney asked. He was a wiry little man, hard as a whipstock with bits of sharp steel for eyes and brown muscle-corded hands. "I wouldn't know him if I saw him."

"Sure, I know him. Big feller, strong made, rusty-like hair an' maybe forty year old. Looks plumb salty, too, an' from what I hear he's no friendly sort of man. Squattin' on that Sorenson place looks plumb suspicious, for no man can make him a livin' on that dry-as-a-bone place. No fit place for man nor beast. Ever'body figures no honest man would squat on such a place."

It seemed a strange thing, to be searching out a man who none of them really knew. Of course, they had all known Johnny Webb. He was a handsome, popular young man, a daredevil and a hellion, but a very attractive one, and a top hand to boot. They had all known him and had all liked him. Then, one of the things that made them so sure that this had been a wrong killing, even aside from the shots in the back, was the fact that Johnny Webb had been the fastest man in the Spring Valley country. Fast, and a dead shot.

Johnny had worked with all these men, and they were good men—hard men, but good. Kimmel, Hardin, and Kesney had all made something of their ranches, as had the others, only somewhat less so. They had come West when the going was rough, fought Indians and rustlers, and then battled drought, dust, and hot, hard winds. It took a strong man to survive in this country, and they had survived. He, Neill, was the youngest of them all and the newest in the country. He was still looked upon with some reserve. He had been here only five years.

Neill could see the tracks of the buckskin, and it gave him a strange feeling to realize that the man who rode that horse would soon be dead, hanging from a noose in one of those ropes attached to a saddle horn of Hardin or Kimmel. Neill had never killed a man or seen one killed by another man, and the thought made him uncomfortable.

Yet Johnny was gone, and his laughter and his jokes were things past. They had brightened more than one roundup, more than one bitter day of heartbreaking labor on the range. Not that he had been an angel. He had been a proper hand with a gun and could throw one. And in his time he had had his troubles.

"He's walkin' his horse," Kesney said, "leadin' him."

"He's a heavy man," Hardin agreed, "an' he figures to give us a long chase."

"Gone lame on him, maybe," Kimmel suggested. "No, that horse isn't limpin'. This Lock is a smart one."

They had walked out of the ankle-deep dust now and were crossing a parched, dry plain of crusted earth. Hardin reined in suddenly and pointed.

"Look there." He indicated a couple of flecks on the face of the earth crust where something had spilled. "Water splashed."

"Careless," Neill said. "He'll need that water."

"No," Kesney said. "He was pourin' water in a cloth to wipe out his horse's nostrils. Bet you a dollar."

"Sure," Hardin agreed, "that's it. Horse breathes a lot better. A man runnin' could kill a good horse on this flat. He knows that."

They rode on, and for almost a half hour no one spoke. Neill frowned at the sun. It had been on his left a few minutes ago, and now they rode straight into it.

"What's he doin'?" Kesney said wonderingly. "This ain't the way to his place!" The trail had turned again, and now the sun was on their right. Then it turned again and was at their backs. Hardin was in the lead, and he drew up and swore wickedly.

They ranged alongside him, and rode down into a draw that cracked the face of the desert alongside the trail they had followed. Below them was a place where a horse had stood, and across the bank something white fluttered from the parched clump of greasewood.

Kesney slid from the saddle and crossed the wash. When he had the slip of white, he stared at it, and then they heard him swear. He walked back and handed it to Hardin. They crowded near.

Neill took the slip from Hardin's fingers after he had read it. It was torn from some sort of book and the words were plain enough, scrawled with a flat rock for a rest.

That was a fair shutin anyways six aint nowhars enuf, go fetch more men. Man on the gray better titen his girth or heel have him a sorebacked hoss.

"Why, that . . . !" Short swore softly. "He was lyin' within fifty yards of us when we come by. Had him a rifle, too. I seen it in a saddle scabbard on that buckskin in town. He could have got one of us, anyway!"

"Two or three most likely," Kimmel commented. The men stared at the paper, and then looked back into the wash. The sand showed a trail, but cattle had walked here, too. It would make the going a little slower.

Neill, his face flushed and his ears red, was tightening his saddle girth. The others avoided his eyes.

The insult to him, even if the advice was good, was an insult to them all. Their jaws tightened. The squatter was playing Indian with them, and none of them liked it.

"Fair shootin', yeah!" Sutter exploded. "Right in the back!"

The trail led down the wash now, and it was slower going. The occasional puffs of wind they had left on the desert above were gone and the heat in the bottom of the wash was oven-like. They rode into it, almost seeming to push their way through flames that seared. Sweat dripped into their eyes until they smarted, and trickled in tiny rivulets through their dust-caked beards, making their faces itch maddeningly.

The wash spilled out into a wide, flat bed of sand left by the rains of bygone years, and the tracks were plainer now. Neill tightened his bandanna and rode on, sodden with heat and weariness. The trail seemed deliberately to lead them into the worst regions, for now he was riding straight toward an alkali lake that loomed ahead.

At the edge of the water, the trail vanished. Lock had ridden right into the lake. They drew up and stared at it, unbelieving.

"He can't cross," Hardin stated flatly. "That's deep out to the middle. Durned treacherous, too. A horse could get bogged down mighty easy."

They skirted the lake, taking it carefully, three going one way, and three the other. Finally, glancing back, Neill caught sight of Kesney's uplifted arm.

"They found it," he said. "Let's go back." Yet, as he rode, he was thinking what they all knew. This was a delay, for Lock knew they would have to scout the shores both ways to find his trail, and there would be a delay while the last three rejoined the first. A small thing, but in such a chase it was important.

"Why not ride right on to the ranch?" Short suggested.

"We might," Hardin speculated. "On the other hand he might fool us an' never go nigh it. Then we could lose him."

The trail became easier, for now Lock was heading straight into the mountains.

"Where's he goin'?" Kesney demanded irritably. "This don't make sense, nohow!"

There was no reply, the horsemen stretching out in single file, riding up the draw into the mountains. Suddenly Kimmel, who was now in the lead, drew up. Before him a thread of water trickled from the rock and spilled into a basin of stones.

"Huh!" Hardin stared. "I never knowed about this spring afore. Might's well have a drink." He swung down.

They all got down, and Neill rolled a smoke.

"Somebody sure fixed her up nice," he said. "That wall of stone makin' that basin ain't so old."

"No, it ain't."

Short watched them drink and grinned.

"He's a fox, right enough. He's an old *ladino*, this one. A reg'lar mossyhorn. It don't take time for one man to drink, an' one hoss. But here we got six men an' six horses to drink an' we lose more time."

"You really think he planned it that way?" Neill was skeptical.

Hardin looked around at him. "Sure. This Lock knows his way around."

When they were riding on, Neill thought about that. Lock *was* shrewd. He was desert wise. And he was leading them a chase. If not even Hardin knew of this spring, and he had been twenty years in the Spring Valley country, then Lock must know a good deal about the country. Of course, this range of mountains was singularly desolate, and there was nothing in them to draw a man.

So they knew this about their quarry. He was a man wise in the ways of desert and trail, and one who knew the country. Also, Neill reflected, it was probable he had built that basin himself. Nobody lived over this way but Lock, for it was not far to the Sorenson place.

Now they climbed a single horse trail across the starkly eroded foothills, sprinkled with clumps of Joshua and Spanish bayonet. It was a weird and broken land, where long fingers of black lava stretched down the hills and out into the desert as though clawing toward the alkali lake they had left behind. The trail mounted steadily and a little breeze touched their cheeks. Neill lifted his hand and wiped dust from his brow and it came away in flakes, plastered by sweat.

The trail doubled and changed, now across the rock face of the burned red sandstone, then into the lava itself, skirting hills where the exposed ledges mounted in layers like a vast cake of many colors. Then the way dipped down, and they wound among huge boulders, smooth as so many water-worn pebbles. Neill sagged in the saddle, for the hours were growing long, and the trail showed no sign of ending.

"Lucky he ain't waitin' to shoot," Kimmel commented, voicing the first remark in over an hour. "He could pick us off like flies."

As if in reply to his comment, there was an angry whine above them, and then the *crack* of a rifle.

As one man they scattered for shelter, whipping rifles from their scabbards, for all but two had replaced them when they reached the lake. Hardin swore, and Kimmel wormed his way to a better view of the country ahead.

Short had left the saddle in his scramble for shelter, and his horse stood in the open, the canteen making a large lump behind the saddle. Suddenly the horse leaped to the solid *thud* of a striking bullet, and then followed the *crack* of the rifle, echoing over the mountainside.

Short swore viciously. "If he killed that horse . . . !" But the horse, while shifting nervously, seemed uninjured.

"Hell!" Kesney yelled. "He shot your canteen!"

It was true enough. Water was pouring onto the ground, and, swearing, Short started to get up. Sutter grabbed his arm.

"Hold it! If he could get that canteen, he could get you!"

They waited, and the trickle of water slowed, then faded to a drip. All of them stared angrily at the unrewarding rocks ahead of them. One canteen the less. Still they had all filled up at the spring and should have enough. Uncomfortably, however, they realized that the object of their chase, the man called Chat Lock, knew where he was taking them, and he had not emptied that canteen by chance. Now they understood the nature of the man they followed. He did nothing without object.

Lying on the sand or rocks they waited, peering ahead.

"He's probably ridin' off now!" Sutter barked.

Nobody showed any disposition to move. The idea appealed to none of them, for the shot into the canteen showed plainly enough the man they followed was no child with a rifle. Kimmel finally put his hat on a rifle muzzle and lifted it. There was no response. Then he tried sticking it around a corner.

Nothing happened, and he withdrew it. Almost at once, a shot hit the trail not far from where the hat had been. The indication was plain. Lock was warning them not only that he was still there, but that he was not to be fooled by so obvious a trick.

They waited, and Hardin suddenly slid over a rock and began a flanking movement. He crawled, and they waited, watching his progress. The cover he had was good, and he could crawl almost to where the hidden marksman must be. Finally he disappeared from their sight, and they waited. Neill tasted the water in his canteen and dozed.

At last they heard a long yell, and, looking up, they saw Hardin standing on a rock far up the trail, waving them on. Mounting, they led Hardin's horse and rode on up the trail. He met them at the trail side, and his eyes were angry.

"Gone!" he said, thrusting out a hard palm. In it lay three brass cartridge shells. "Found 'em standing up in a line on a rock. An' look here." He pointed, and they stared down at the trail where he indicated. A neat arrow made of stones pointed down the trail ahead of them, and scratches on the face of the sandstone above it were the words:

FOLLER THE SIGNS

Kesney jerked his hat from his head and hurled it to the ground.

"Why, that dirty . . . !" He stopped, beside himself with anger. The contempt of the man they pursued was obvious. He was making fools of them, deliberately teasing them, indicating his trail as to a child or a tenderfoot.

"That ratty back-shootin' killer!" Short said. "I'll take pleasure in usin' a rope on him! Thinks he's smart!"

They started on, and the horse ahead of them left a plain trail, but a quarter of a mile farther along three dried pieces of mesquite had been laid in the trail to form another arrow.

Neill stared at it. This was becoming a personal matter now. He was deliberately playing with them, and he must know how that would set with men such as Kimmel and Hardin. It was a deliberate challenge; more, it was a sign of the utmost contempt.

The vast emptiness of the basin they skirted now was becoming lost in the misty purple light of late afternoon. On the right, the wall of the mountain grew steeper and turned a deeper red. The burned red of the earlier hours was now a bright rust red, and here and there long fingers of quartz shot their white arrows down into the face of the cliff.

They all saw the next message, but all read and averted their eyes. It was written on a blank face of the cliff. First, there was an arrow, pointing ahead, and then the words:

SHADE, SO YOU DON'T GIT SUNSTROK

They rode on, and for several miles, as the shadows drew down, they followed the markers their quarry left at intervals along the trail. All six of the men were tired and beaten. Their horses moved slowly, and the desert air was growing chill. It had been a long chase.

Suddenly Kimmel and Kesney, who rode side-by-side, reined in. A small wall of rock was across the trail, and an arrow pointed downward into a deep cleft.

"What do you think, Hardin? He could pick us off man by man."

Hardin studied the situation with misgivings and hesitated, lighting a smoke.

"He ain't done it yet."

Neill's remark fell into the still air like a rock into a calm pool of water. As the rings of ripples spread wider into the thoughts of the other five, he waited.

Lock could have killed one or two of them, perhaps all of them by now. Why had he not? Was he waiting for darkness and an easy getaway? Or was he leading them into a trap?

"The devil with it!" Hardin exclaimed impatiently. He wheeled his horse and, pistol in hand, started down into the narrow rift in the dark. One by one, they followed. The darkness closed around them, and the air was damp and chill. They rode on, and then the trail mounted steeply toward a grayness ahead of them, and they came out in a small basin. Ahead of them they heard a trickle of running water and saw the darkness of trees.

Cautiously they approached. Suddenly they saw the light of a fire. Hardin drew up sharply and slid from his horse. The others followed. In a widening circle, they crept toward the fire. Kesney was the first to reach it, and the sound of his swearing rent the stillness and shattered it like thin glass. They swarmed in around him.

The fire was built close beside a small running stream, and nearby was a neat pile of dry sticks. On a paper, laid out carefully on a rock, was a small mound of coffee, and another of sugar. Nobody said anything for a minute, staring at the fire and the coffee. The taunt was obvious, and they were bitter men. It was bad enough to have a stranger make such fools of them on a trail, to treat them like tenderfeet, but to prepare a camp for them. . . .

"I'll be cussed if I will!" Short said violently. "I'll go sleep on the desert first!"

"Well. . . ." Hardin was philosophical. "Might's well make the most of it. We can't trail him at night, no way."

Kimmel had dug a coffee pot out of his pack and was getting water from the stream that flowed from a basin just above the camp. Several of the others began to dig out grub, and Kesney sat down glumly, staring into the fire. He started to pick a stick off the pile left for them, and then jerked his hand as though he had seen a snake. Getting up, he stalked back into the trees, and, after a minute, he returned.

Sutter was looking around, and suddenly he spoke. "Boys, I know this place! Only I never knew about that crack in the wall. This here's the Mormon Well!"

Hardin sat up and looked around. "Durned if it ain't," he said. "I ain't been in here for six or seven years."

Sutter squatted on his haunches. "Look!" He was excited and eager, sketching with a stick in the sand. "Here's Mormon Well, where we are. Right over here to the northwest there's an old sawmill an' a tank just above it. I'll bet a side of beef that durned killer is holed up for the night in that sawmill!"

Kesney, who had taken most to heart the taunting of the man they pursued, was on his knees, staring at the diagram drawn in the damp sand. He was nodding thoughtfully.

"He's right! He sure is. I remember that old mill! I holed up there one time in a bad storm. Spent two days in it. If that sidewinder stays there tonight, we can get him!"

As they ate, they talked over their plan. Traveling over the rugged mountains ahead of them was almost impossible in the darkness, and, besides, even if Lock could go the night without stopping, his horse could not. The buckskin must have a rest. Moreover, with all the time Lock had been losing along the trail, he could not be far ahead. It stood to reason that he must have planned just this, for them to stop here, and to hole up in the sawmill himself.

"We'd better surprise him," Hardin suggested. "That sawmill is heavy timber, an' a man in there with a rifle an' plenty of ammunition could stand us off for a week."

"Has he got plenty?"

"Sure he has," Neill told them. "I was in the Bon Ton when he bought his stuff. He's got grub and he's got plenty of Forty-Fours. They do for either his Colt or his Winchester."

Unspoken as yet, but present in the mind of each man, was a growing respect for their quarry, a respect and an element of doubt. Would such a man as this shoot another in the back? The evidence against him was plain enough, or seemed plain enough.

Yet beyond the respect there was something else, for it was no longer simply a matter of justice to be done, but a personal thing. Each of them felt in some measure that his reputation was at stake. It had not been enough for Lock to leave an obvious trail, but he must leave markers, the sort to be used for any tenderfoot. There were men in this group who could trail a wood tick through a pine forest.

"Well," Kimmel said reluctantly and somewhat grimly, "he left us good coffee, anyway."

They tried the coffee and agreed. Few things in this world are so comforting and so warming to the heart as hot coffee on a chilly night over a campfire when the day has been long and weary. They drank, and they relaxed. And as they relaxed, the seeds of doubt began to sprout and put forth branches of speculation.

"He could have got more'n one of us today," Sutter hazarded. "This one is brush wise."

"I'll pull that rope on him!" Short stated positively. "No man makes a fool out of me." But in his voice there was something lacking.

"You know," Kesney suggested, "if he knows these hills like he seems to, an' if he really wanted to lose us, we'd have to burn the stump and sift the ashes before we found him."

There was no reply. Hardin drew back and eased the

leg of his pants away from the skin, for the cloth had grown too hot for comfort.

Short tossed a stick from the neat pile into the fire. "That mill ain't so far away," he suggested. "Shall we give her a try?"

"Later." Hardin leaned back against a log and yawned. "She's been a hard day."

"Both them bullets go in Johnny's back?"

The question moved among them like a ghost. Short stirred uneasily, and Kesney looked up and glared around. "Sure they did! Didn't they, Hardin?"

"Sure." He paused thoughtfully. "Well, no. One of them was under his left arm. Right between the ribs. Looked like a heart shot to me. The other one went through near his spine."

"The hell with it," Kesney declared. "No slick, rustlin' squatter can come into this country and shoot one of our boys. He was shot in the back, an' I seen both holes. Johnny got that one nigh the spine, an' he must have turned and tried to draw, then got that bullet through the heart."

Nobody had seen it. Neill remembered that, and the thought rankled. Were they doing an injustice? He felt like a traitor at the thought, but secretly he had acquired a strong tinge of respect for the man they followed.

The fire flickered and the shadows danced a slow, rhythmic quadrille against the dark background of trees. He peeled bark from the log beside him and fed it into the fire. It caught, sparked brightly, and popped once or twice. Hardin leaned over and pushed the coffee pot nearer the coals. Kesney checked the loads in his Winchester.

"How far to that sawmill, Hardin?"

"About six miles, the way we go."

"Let's get started." Short got to his feet and brushed off the sand. "I want to get home. Got my boys buildin' fence. You either keep a close watch or they are off gal hootin' over the hills."

They tightened their saddle girths, doused the fire, and mounted up. With Hardin in the lead once more, they moved off into the darkness.

Neill brought up the rear. It was damp and chill among the cliffs and felt like the inside of a cavern. Overhead the stars were very bright. Mary was going to be worried, for he was never home so late. Nor did he like leaving her alone. He wanted to be home, eating a warm supper and going to bed in the old four-poster with the patchwork quilt Mary's grand-mother had made pulled over him. What enthusiasm he had had for the chase was gone. The warm fire, the coffee, his own weariness, and the growing respect for Lock had changed him.

Now they all knew he was not the manner of man they had supposed. Justice can be a harsh taskmaster, but Western men know their kind, and the lines were strongly drawn. When you have slept beside a man on the trail, worked with him and with others like him, you come to know your kind. In the trail of the man

Chat Lock, each rider of the posse was seeing the sort of man he knew, the sort he could respect. The thought was nagging and insubstantial, but each of them felt a growing doubt, even Short and Kesney, who were most obdurate and resentful.

They knew how a back-shooter lived and worked. He had his brand on everything he did. The mark of this man was the mark of a man who did things, who stood upon his own two feet, and who, if he died, died facing his enemy. To the unknowing, such conclusions might seem doubtful, but the men of the desert knew their kind.

The mill was dark and silent, a great looming hulk beside the stream and the still pool of the millpond. They dismounted and eased close. Then, according to a prearranged plan, they scattered and surrounded it. From behind a lodgepole pine, Hardin called out.

"We're comin' in, Lock! We want you!"

The challenge was harsh and ringing. Now that the moment had come, something of the old suspense returned. They listened to the water babbling as it trickled over the old dam, and then they moved. At their first step, they heard Lock's voice.

"Don't you come in here, boys! I don't want to kill none of you, but you come an' I will! That was a fair shootin'! You've got no call to come after me!"

Hardin hesitated, chewing his mustaches. "You shot him in the back!" he yelled.

"No such thing! He was a-facin' the bar when I come in. He seen I was heeled, an' he drawed as he

99

turned. I beat him to it. My first shot took him in the side an' he was knocked back against the bar. My second hit him in the back, an' the third missed as he was a-fallin'. You *hombres* didn't see that fight."

The sound of his voice trailed off, and the water chuckled over the stones and then sighed to a murmur among the trees. The logic of Lock's statement struck them all. It *could* have been that way.

A long moment passed, and then Hardin spoke up again.

"You come in and we'll give you a trial. Fair an' square."

"How?" Lock's voice was a challenge. "You ain't got no witness. Neither have I. Ain't nobody to say what happened there but me, as Johnny ain't alive."

"Johnny was a mighty good man, an' he was our friend!" Short shouted. "No murderin' squatter is goin' to move into this country an' start shootin' folks up!"

There was no reply to that, and they waited, hesitating a little. Neill leaned disconsolately against the tree where he stood. After all, Lock might be telling the truth. How did they know? There was no use hanging a man unless you were sure.

"Gab!" Short's comment was explosive. "Let's move in, Hardin! Let's get him! He's lyin'! Nobody could beat Johnny, we know that!"

"Webb was a good man in his own country!" Lock shouted in reply. The momentary silence that followed held them, and then, almost as a man they began moving in. Neill did not know exactly when or why he started. Inside, he felt sick and empty. He was fed up on the whole business, and every instinct told him this man was no back-shooter.

Carefully they moved, for they knew this man was handy with a gun. Suddenly Hardin's voice rang out.

"Hold it, men! Stay where you are until daybreak! Keep your eyes open an' your ears. If he gets out of here, he'll be lucky, an' in the daylight we can get him, or fire the mill!"

Neill sank to a sitting position behind a log. Relief was a great warmth that swept over him. There wouldn't be any killing tonight. Not tonight, at least.

Yet, as the hours passed, his ears grew more and more attuned to the darkness. A rabbit rustled, a pinecone dropped from a tree, the wind stirred high in the pine tops, and the few stars winked through, lonesomely peering down upon the silent men.

With daylight they moved in and they went through the doors and up to the windows of the old mill, and it was empty and still. They stared at each other, and Short swore viciously, the sound booming in the echoing, empty room.

"Let's go down to the Sorenson place," Kimmel said. "He'll be there."

And somehow they were all very sure he would be. They knew he would be because they knew him for their kind of man. He would retreat no farther than his own ranch, his own hearth. There, if they were to have him and hang him, they would have to burn him out, and men would die in the process. Yet with these men there was no fear. They felt the drive of duty, the need for maintaining some law in this lonely desert and mountain land. There was only doubt that had grown until each man was shaken with it. Even Short, who the markers by the trail had angered, and Kesney, who was the best tracker among them, even better than Hardin, had been irritated by it, too.

The sun was up and warming them when they rode over the brow of the hill and looked down into the parched basin where the Sorenson place lay.

But it was no parched basin. Hardin drew up so suddenly his startled horse almost reared. It was no longer the Sorenson place.

The house had been patched and rebuilt. The roof had spots of new lumber upon it, and the old pole barn had been made watertight and strong. A new corral had been built, and to the right of the house was a fenced-in garden of vegetables, green and pretty after the desert of the day before.

Thoughtfully, and in a tight cavalcade, they rode down the hill. The stock they saw was fat and healthy and the corral was filled with horses.

"Been a lot of work done here," Kimmel said. And he knew how much work it took to make such a place attractive.

"Don't look like no killer's place!" Neill burst out Then he flushed and drew back, embarrassed by his statement. He was the youngest of these men and the newest in the country.

No response was forthcoming. He had but stated what they all believed. There was something stable and lasting and something real and genuine in this place.

"I been waitin' for you."

The remark from behind them stiffened every spine. Chat Lock was here, behind them. And he would have a gun on them, and, if one of them moved, he could die.

"My wife's down there fixin' breakfast. I told her I had some friends comin' in. A posse huntin' a killer. I've told her nothin' about this trouble. You ride down there now, you keep your guns. You eat your breakfast, and then, if you feel bound and determined to get somebody for a fair shootin', I'll come out with anyone of you or all of you, but I ain't goin' to hang. I ain't namin' no one man because I don't want to force no fight on anybody. You ride down there now."

They rode, and in the dooryard they dismounted. Neill turned then, and for the first time he saw Chat Lock.

He was a big man, compact and strong. His rusty brown hair topped a brown, sun-hardened face, but with the warmth in his eyes it was a friendly sort of face. Not at all what he expected.

Hardin looked at him. "You made some changes here."

"I reckon." Lock gestured toward the well. "Dug by

hand. My wife worked the windlass." He looked around at them, taking them in with one sweep of his eyes. "I've got the grandest woman in the world."

Neill felt hot tears in his eyes suddenly and busied himself loosening his saddle girth to keep the others from seeing. That was the way he felt about Mary.

The door opened suddenly, and they turned. The sight of a woman in this desert country was enough to make any man turn. What they saw was not what they expected. She was young, perhaps in her middle twenties, and she was pretty, with brown wavy hair and gray eyes and a few freckles on her nose. "Won't you come in? Chat told me he had some friends coming for breakfast, and it isn't often we have anybody in."

Heavy-footed and shamefaced they walked up on the porch. Kesney saw the care and neatness with which the hard-hewn planks had been fitted. Here, too, was the same evidence of lasting, of permanence, of strength. This was the sort of man a country needed. He thought the thought before he fixed his attention on it, and then he flushed.

Inside, the room was as neat as the girl herself. How did she get the floors so clean? Before he thought, he phrased the question. She smiled.

"Oh, that was Chat's idea. He made a frame and fastened a piece of pumice stone to a stick. It cuts into all the cracks and keeps them very clean."

The food smelled good, and, when Hardin looked at his hands, Chat motioned to the door.

"There's water an' towels if you want to wash up."

Neill rolled up his sleeves and dipped his hands in the basin. The water was soft, and that was rare in this country, and the soap felt good on his hands. When he had dried his hands, he walked in. Hardin and Kesney had already seated themselves, and Lock's wife was pouring coffee.

"Men," Lock said, "this is Mary. You'll have to tell her your names. I reckon I missed them."

Mary. Neill looked up. She was Mary, too. He looked down at his plate again and ate a few bites. When he looked up, she was smiling at him.

"My wife's name is Mary," he said. "She's a fine girl."

"She would be. But why don't you bring her over? I haven't talked with a woman in so long I wouldn't know how it seemed. Chat, why haven't you invited them over?"

Chat mumbled something, and Neill stared at his coffee. The men ate in uncomfortable silence. Hardin's eyes kept shifting around the room. That pumice stone. He'd have to fix up a deal like that for Jane. She was always fussing about the work of keeping a board floor clean. That washstand inside, too, with pipes made of hollow logs to carry the water out so she wouldn't have to be running back and forth. That was an idea, too.

They finished their meal reluctantly. One by one they trooped outside, avoiding each other's eyes. Chat Lock did not keep them waiting. He walked down among them.

"If there's to be shootin'," he said quietly, "let's get away from the house."

Hardin looked up. "Lock, was that right, what you said at the mill? Was it a fair shootin'?"

Lock nodded. "It was. Johnny Webb prodded me. I didn't want trouble, nor did I want to hide behind the fact I wasn't packin' an iron. I walked over to the saloon, not aimin' for trouble. I aimed to give him a chance if he wanted it. He drawed, an' I beat him. It was a fair shootin'."

"All right." Hardin nodded. "That's good enough for me. I reckon you're a different sort of man than any of us figured."

"Let's mount up," Short said. "I got fence to build."

Chat Lock put his hand on Hardin's saddle. "You folks come over sometime. She gets right lonesome. I don't mind it so much, but you know how women folks are."

"Sure," Hardin said, "sure thing."

"An' you bring your Mary over," he told Neill.

Neill nodded, his throat full. As they mounted the hill, he glanced back. Mary Lock was standing in the doorway, waving to them, and the sunlight was very bright in the clean-swept dooryard.

The Rider of Lost Creek

I

A lone cowhand riding a hard-pressed horse reined in at the hitching rail before a Dodge barroom. Swinging from saddle, he pushed through the batwing doors, slapping the dust from his hat.

"Make it rye," he said hoarsely, as he reached the bar.

When the raw, harsh liquor had cut the dust from his throat, he looked up at a nearby customer, a man known throughout the West as a gun expert—Phil Coe.

"They've begun it," he said, his voice rough with feeling. "They're puttin' wire on the range in Texas."

"Wire?" A burly cattle buyer straightened up and glared. "Huh, they won't dare! Wire ain't practical! This here's a free range country, and it'll always be free range!"

"Don't make no difference," the cowhand who had just entered insisted grimly. "They're a-doin' it." He downed a second shot, shuddered, then glanced up slantwise at Coe. "You seen Kilkenny?"

He spoke softly, but a hush seemed to fall over the room, and men's eyes sought each other questioningly. Somewhere chips clicked, emphasizing the stillness, the listening.

"No," Coe said after a minute, "and you better not go around askin' for him."

"I got to see him," the cowpuncher insisted stubbornly. "I been sent to find him, and I got to do my job."

"What you want with Kilkenny?" demanded a short, wide-faced young man with light hair and narrow, pig-like eyes.

The cowpuncher glanced at him and his own eyes darkened. Death, he knew, was never far away when anybody talked to this man. Along with Roya Barnes, Wild Bill Hickok, and Kilkenny himself, this Wes Hardin was one of the most feared men in the West. He was said to be fast as Hickok and as cold-blooded as the Brockman twins.

"They want guns in the Live Oak country, Hardin," the cowpuncher said. "There's a range war comin'."

"Then don't look for Kilkenny," Coe said. "He rides alone, and his gun ain't for hire."

"You seen him?" the cowpuncher persisted. "I got word for him from an old friend of his."

"I hear tell he tied up with King Fisher," someone said.

"Don't you believe it," the cattle buyer stated flatly. "He don't tie up with nobody." He hesitated, then glanced at the cowpuncher. "I did hear tell he was down in the Indian Territory a while back."

"Who'd you get the word from?" Coe asked the cowpuncher quietly. "Might be somebody here knows Kilkenny and could pass the word along."

"Just say Mort Davis is in trouble. Kilkenny won' need no more than that. He sticks by his friends."

"That's right." The cattle buyer nodded emphatically. "Mort nursed him through a bad time after Kilkenny gunned down the three Webers. Mort stood off the gang that come to lynch Kilkenny. Iffen Kilkenny hears Mort needs help, he'll ride."

"Funny Royal Barnes never hunted Kilkenny for killin' the Webers," someone suggested. "With Barnes bein' half-brother to the Webers and all."

"That'd be somethin' . . . Barnes an' Kilkenny," another agreed. "Two of the fastest gunmen in the West."

Conversation flowered in the room, and through it all the name of Kilkenny was woven like a scarlet thread. One man had seen him in Abilene. Two men had cornered him there, two bad men trying to build a tough reputation. They had drawn, but both had died before they could fire a shot. Another man said he had seen Kilkenny hold his hand out at arm's length with a poker chip on its back. Then he had tipped his hand slowly, and, when the chip fell free, he had drawn and fired before the chip reached the level of his waist.

"He's faster'n Hickok," someone else said dogmatically, "and he's got the nerve of Ben Thompson."

"What's he look like?" still another demanded. "I never seen the feller."

"Nobody agrees," the cattle buyer said. "I've heard a dozen descriptions of Kilkenny, and no two alike. He never makes hisself known until the guns start shootin', and he fades right after. Nobody knows him."

"This wire won't last in Texas," a lean, raw-boned Texan changed the subject to say. "That Live Oaks country nor this 'n', either, they ain't made for wire. It's free range and always will be. The buffalo was here before the longhorn, and it was free grass then. It always has been."

"I don't know," someone else said doubtfully. "There's farmers comin' out from the East. Hoemen who'll fence their own ground and break the sod for crops."

"This country ain't right for farmin', I tell you," a young cowhand said. "You ever foller a trail herd? Iffen they ever plow this plains country up, it will blow clean to Mexico!"

But even as the men in Dodge talked and condemned wires, along the right way in Botalla, in the Live Oak country, lay huge reels of it, gleaming and new. Literally miles of it, on great spools, unloaded from wagon trains and ready to be strung. Reports implied there would soon be a railroad in Texas. Fat beef, good beef, would soon be in great demand. In this year of 1880, 40,000 tons of steel barbed wire of the Haish and Glidden Star varieties were to be sold to Texas ranchmen.

In the bar of the old Trail House in Botalla, rancher Webb Steele smashed a ham-like fist upon the bar. "We're puttin' it up!" he shouted. "Hoss high, pig tight, and bull strong! If them who don't like it want war, it's war they'll get!"

"Who fences Lost Creek Valley?" some hardened soul demanded. "You or Chet Lord?"

"I'm fencin' it!" Steele declared, glaring about the room. "And if necessary my riders will ride the fence with rifles!"

Outside the barroom a tall man in black trousers, black shirt, and a worn buckskin vest walked a rangy yellow horse down the one street of Botalla, then swung down in front of the Trail House. The buckskin relaxed, standing tree-legged, head hanging in weariness. The tall man loosened the cinch, taking in the street with quick, alert eyes.

It was merely the usual double row of false fronted buildings he saw, almost every other one a saloon. He knew that men along the walk were looking at him, wondering about him, but he seemed not to notice.

He could feel their eyes, though, like a tangible touch, lifting from his low-slung, tied-down guns to his lean brown face and green eyes. They were noting the dust in the grain of his face, the dust on his clothing, the dust on the long-legged buckskin. They would know he had traveled far and fast, and that would mean he had traveled for a reason.

When he stepped up on the walk, he closed his eyes for an instant. It was a trick he had learned that would leave his eyes accustomed to inner dimness much more quickly than would otherwise be the case. Then he stepped through the doors, letting his eyes shift from left to right, taking in the room in one swift, comprehensive glance. There was no one he knew. No one here, he was sure, knew him.

Webb Steele, brawny and huge, strode past him

through the doors, his guns seeming small, buckled to his massive frame.

"I'll have a whiskey," the tall man said to the bartender. He took off his flat-crowned black hat to run his fingers around the sweaty band, then through his black curly hair. He replaced the hat, dropped his right hand to the bar, then glanced about.

Several men leaned on the bar nearby. The nearest, a man who had walked to the bar as Steele left, was a slim, wiry young fellow in a fringed buckskin jacket and black jeans stuffed into cowhide boots.

The young man had gray, cold eyes. He looked hard at the stranger. "Don't I know you?" he demanded.

The green eyes lifted in a direct expressionless look. "You might."

"Ridin' through?"

"Mebbe."

"Want a job?"

"Mebbe."

"Ain't you a cowhand?"

"Sometimes."

"I'll pay well."

"What outfit you with?"

"I'm not with any outfit," the young man said sharply. "I *am* the Tumblin' R."

"Yeah?"

The young man's face flamed and a queer, white eagerness came into his eyes. "I don't like the way you said that!" he snapped.

"Does it matter?" drawled the tall man. For an

instant the young rancher stared as if he couldn't believe his ears, and he heard men hurriedly backing away from him. Something turned over inside him, and with a sickening sensation in the pit of his stomach he realized with startling clarity that he was facing a gun battle, out in the open and alone.

An icy chill went down his spine. Always before when he had talked, loud and free, the fact that he was Chet Lord's son had saved him. Men knew his hard-bitten old father only too well. Then, there had been Bonner and Swindell. Those two men had affronted Steve Lord and later both had been found dead in the trail, gun in hand.

Suddenly the awful realization that he must fight swept over Steve Lord. Nothing his father might do afterward would do any good now. He stiffened. His face was tense and white as he stared into the cold green eyes of the stranger.

"Yeah," he snapped, "it matters, and I'll make it matter!"

His hand hovered over his gun. For an instant, the watchers held their breaths. The tall man at the bar stared at Steve Lord coolly, then Steve saw those hard green eyes change, and a glint of humor and friendliness came into them.

With a shrug the stranger turned away. "Well," he drawled, "don't kill me now. I hate to get shot on an empty stomach." Deliberately he turned his back and looked at the bartender. "How about another whiskey? The trail shore does make a feller dry."

Everyone began talking suddenly, and Steve Lord, astonished and relieved, dropped his hand to his side. Something had happened to him and all he knew was that he had narrowly escaped death from a shoot-out with a man to whom blazing guns were not new.

The tall man at the bar lifted his eyes to the mirror in time to see a thin-bodied fellow with close-set eyes slide quietly from his chair and go out the side door. No one seemed to notice him go except the tall stranger who noted the intentness of the man's eyes, and something sly in his movements.

The stranger swallowed his drink, turned on his heel, and walked outside. The thin man who had left the Trail House was talking with three men across the street in front of the Spur Saloon. The tall man saw the eyes of the three pick him up. Swiftly screening their faces, he strolled on.

Idling in front of the empty stage station a few minutes later, he saw Steve Lord coming toward him. Something about the young man disturbed him, but although his eyes lifted from the cigarette he was rolling, he said nothing when Steve stopped before him.

"You could have killed me," Steve said sharply staring at him.

"Yeah." The tall stranger smiled a little.

"Why didn't you? I made a fool of myself, talkin' too much."

The stranger smiled. "No use killin' a man unnecessarily. You may be Chet Lord's son as I heard, but I think you make your own tracks."

"Thanks. That's the first time anybody ever said that to me."

"Mebbe they should have." The stranger took a long drag, and glanced sideward at Steve. "Knowin' you're pretty much of a man often helps a feller be one."

"Who are you?" asked Steve Lord.

The stranger shrugged. "The name is Lance," he replied slowly. "Is that enough for you?"

"Yeah. About that job. We'd like to have you. I may not be gun slick but I know when a man is."

"I don't reckon I'll go to work just now," observed the man who said his name was Lance.

"I'd rather have you on our side than the other," Steve said honestly. "And we'll pay well."

"Mebbe I won't ride for either side."

"You got to! Those that ain't for us are against us."

Lance smoked quietly for a moment. "Tell me," he finally said, "what kind of a scrap is this?"

"It's a three-cornered scrap actually," Steve said. "Our outfit has about forty riders, and Webb Steele has about the same number. We split the Live Oak country between us. By the Live Oak, I mean the territory between the two ranges of hills you see out east and west of here. They taper down to a point at the border. Webb Steele and us Lords both have started puttin' up wire, and no trouble till we get to Lost Creek Valley, the richest piece of it all. Good grass there, and lots of water."

"You said it was three-cornered. Who's the other corner?"

"He don't matter so much." Steve shrugged. "The real fight is between the two big outfits. This other corner is a feller name of Mort Davis. Squatter. He come in here about three year ago with his family and squatted on the Wagontire water hole. We cut his wire, and he cut ours. There she stands right now."

Lance studied the street thoughtfully, aware that while he was talking with Steve Lord, something was building up down there. Something that smelled like trouble. The three men with whom the thin man had talked had scattered. One was watching a boy unloading some feed, one was leaning on the hitch rail, another was studying some faded medicine show posters in a window.

Abruptly Lance turned away from Steve. There was something behind this, and he intended to know what. If they wanted him, they could have him.

II

Lance had started strolling carelessly toward the Spur Saloon when he heard a sudden rattle of wheels and racing hoofs behind him, and sprang aside just in time to escape being run down by a madly careening buckboard. The driver—a girl—stood up, sawing the plunging broncos to a halt, then wheeling the buckboard to race them back at a spanking trot. She

116

brought them up alongside of Lance and her eyes were ablaze with irritation.

"Will you please stay out of the street?" she demanded icily.

Lance looked at her steadily. Red-gold hair blew in the wind, and her eyes were an amazingly deep blue. She was beautiful, not merely pretty, and there was in her eyes the haughty disdain of a queen who reprimands a clumsy subject.

"Pretty," he drawled slowly, "pretty, but plumb spoiled. Could be quite a lady, too," he added regretfully. Then he smiled and removed his hat. "Sorry, ma'am. If you'll let me know when you expect to use the street for a racetrack, I'll keep out of the way. I'll do my best to keep everybody else out of the way, too."

He turned as if to go, but her voice halted him. "Wait!"

She took a couple of quick turns with the lines, jumped to the street, and marched up to him. Her eyes were arrogant and her nostrils tight with anger. "Did you mean to insinuate that I wasn't a lady?" she demanded. She held her horsewhip in her right hand, and he could see she intended to use it.

He smiled again. "I did," he said quietly. "You see, ma'am, it takes more than just beauty and a little money to make a lady. A lady is thoughtful of other people. A lady don't go racing around running people down with a buckboard, and, when she does come close, she comes back and apologizes."

Her eyes grew darker and darker and he could see the coldness of fury in them. "You," she snapped contemptuously, "a common cowpuncher, trying to tell me how to be a lady!"

She drew back the whip and struck furiously, but he was expecting it, and without even shifting his feet he threw up an arm and blocked the blow of the whip with his forearm. Then he dropped his hand over and grasped the whip. With a quick twist he jerked it from her hands.

The movement tilted her off balance and she fell forward into his arms. He caught her, looked down into her upturned face, into her eyes blazing with astonishment and frustrated anger, and at her parted lips. He smiled. "I'd kiss you," he drawled, "and you look invitin', and most like it would be a lot of fun, but I won't. You spirited kind kiss much better if you come and ask for it."

"Ask?" She tore herself free from him, trembling from head to foot. "I'd never kiss you if you were the last man alive."

"No, ma'am, I reckon not. You'd be standin' in line waitin', standin' away back."

A hard voice behind Lance stopped him short.

"Seems like you're takin' in a lot of territory around here, stranger. I'd like to ask you a few questions."

Lance turned slowly, careful to hold his hands away from his guns.

The thin-faced man was standing close by, his thumbs hooked in his belt. Two of the other men had spread out, one right and one left. The third man was out of sight, had circled behind him probably, or was across the buckboard from him.

"Let's have the questions," he replied calmly. "I'm right curious myself."

"I want to know," the man demanded, his eyes narrow and ugly, "where you was day before yesterday."

Lance was puzzled. "The day before yesterday? I was ridin' a good many miles from here. Why?"

"You got witnesses?" the thin man sneered. "You better have."

"What you gettin' at?" Lance demanded.

"I s'pose you claim you never heard of Joe Wilkins?"

Several men had gathered around now. Lance could hear them muttering among themselves at the mention of that name.

"What do you mean?" Lance asked. "Who is Joe Wilkins?"

"He was killed on Lost Creek trail the day before yesterday," the fellow snapped. "You was on that trail then, and there's them that think you done him in. You deny it?"

"Deny it?" Lance stared at the man, his eyes watchful. "Why, I never heard of Joe Wilkins, haven't any reason to kill him. 'Course, I haven't seen him."

"They found Wilkins," the thin man went on, his cruel eyes fastened on Lance, "drilled between the eyes. Shot with a six-gun. You was on that road, and he'd been carryin' money. You robbed him."

Lance watched the man steadily. There was something more behind this bald accusation than appeared on the surface. Either an effort was being made to force him to make a break so they could kill him, or the effort was to discredit him. If he made a flat denial, it would be considered that he was calling the fellow a liar, and probably would mean a shoot-out. Lance chuckled carelessly. "How'd you know I was on Lost Creek trail?"

"I seen you," the man declared.

"Then," Lance said gently, "you were on the trail, too. Or you were off it, because I didn't see you. If you were off the trail, you were hiding, and, if so, why? Did you kill this Wilkins?"

The man's eyes narrowed to slits, and suddenly Lance sensed a hint of panic in them. They had expected him to say something to invite a fight. Instead, he had turned the accusation on his accuser.

"No! I didn't kill him!" the man declared. "He was my friend!"

"Never noticed you bein' so friendly with him, Polti," a big farmer declared. "If you was, I don't think he knowed it."

"You shut up," Polti, the thin man, snapped, his eyes blazing. "I'll do the talkin' here."

"You talked enough," Lance replied calmly, "to make somebody right suspicious. Why are you so durned anxious to pin this killin' on a stranger?"

"You killed Wilkins," Polti growled harshly, and

triumph shone in his eyes. "Somebody search his sad-dlebags! You all knew Wilkins had him some gold dust he used to carry around. I bet we'll find it."

"You seem right shore," Lance suggested. "Did you put it in my bag while I was in the Trail House? I saw you slippin' out."

"Tryin' to get out of it?" Polti sneered. "Well, you won't. I'm goin' to search them bags here and now."

Lance was very still, and his green eyes turned hard and cold. "No," he said flatly. "If anybody searches them bags, it won't be you, and it'll be done in the presence of witnesses."

"I'll search 'em!" Polti snapped. "Now!"

He wheeled, but before he could take even one step, Lance moved. He grabbed the thin man and spun him around. With a whining cry of fury, Polti went for his gun, but his hand never reached the holster. Lance's left hit Polti's chin with a crack like that of a black-snake whip, and Polti sagged. A left and a right smashed him down, bleeding from the mouth.

"This don't look so good for you, stranger," the big farmer stated fearlessly. "Let's look at them bags."

"Right," Lance replied quietly. "An honest man ain't got anything to fear, they say, but it wouldn't surprise me none to find the dust there."

Watching him closely, the crowd, augmented now by a dozen more, followed him to his horse. Suddenly he stopped.

"No," he said, "a man might palm it if it's small." He turned to the girl who had driven the buckboard, and who now stood nearby. "Ma'am, my apologies for our earlier difficulty, and will you go through the bags for me?"

Her eyes snapped. "With pleasure! And hope I find the evidence!"

She removed the articles from the saddlebags one by one. They were few enough. Two boxes of .45 ammunition, one of rifle ammunition, some cleaning materials, and a few odds and ends of rawhide.

As she drew the packet of pictures out, one of them slipped from the packet and fell to the ground. The girl stopped quickly and retrieved it, glancing curiously at the picture of an elderly woman with a face of quiet dignity and poise. For an instant she glanced at Lance, then looked away.

"There is no gold here," she said quietly. "None at all."

"Well," Lance said, and turned, "I guess. . . ."

Polti was gone.

"Puts you in the clear, stranger," the big farmer said. "I wonder where it leaves Polti?"

"Mebbe he'd've tried to slip it into the saddlebag when he searched it," somebody suggested. "Wouldn't put it past him."

Lance glanced at the speaker. "That implies he has the gold dust. If he has, he probably killed Wilkins."

Nobody spoke, and Lance glanced from one to the other. A few men at the rear of the crowd began to sidle away. Finally the big farmer looked up.

"Well, nobody is goin' to say Jack Pickett lacks

nerve," he said, "but I ain't goin' to tackle Polti and them gun-slick *hombres* he trails with. It's like askin' for it."

The crowd dwindled, and Lance turned to find the golden-haired girl still standing there.

"I'm still not sure," she said coldly. "You could have buried it."

He grinned. "That's right, ma'am, I could have."

He turned and walked away. The girl stared after him, her brows knit.

Lance led the buckskin slowly down the street to the livery stable. He walked because he wanted to think, and he thought well on his feet. This thing had a lot of angles. Polti was mean and cruel. The man was obviously a killer who would stop at nothing. For some reason he had deliberately started out to frame Lance. Why, there seemed no reason. He might, of course, know why he had come to Live Oak and the town of Botalla.

In the livery stable Lance was rubbing down the buckskin when he heard a voice speak from the darkness of a stall behind him.

"Busy little feller, ain't you?"

The speaker stepped out of the stall into the light. He wore a battered hat, patched jeans, and a hickory shirt. Yet the guns on his hips looked business-like. Powerfully built, he had brick-red hair, and a glint of humor in his sardonic blue eyes.

"Name of Gates," he said. "They call me Rusty."

"I'm Lance."

The eyes of the stranger in Botalla took in the cow-puncher with quick intelligence. This man was rugged and capable. He looked as if he would do to ride the river with.

"So I heard." Rusty began making a smoke. Then he looked up, grinning. "Like I say, you're busy. You invite Steve Lord to a shootin' party, then side-step and let him off easy. A lot of people are askin' why. They want to know if you've throwed in with Chet Lord. They want to know if you was scared out. Then you tangle with that wildcat, Tana Steele. . . ."

"Webb Steele's daughter? I thought so. Noticed the name of Tana Steele on a package in the buckboard."

"Yeah. That's her, and trouble on wheels, pard. She'll never forgive, and, before she's through, she'll make you eat your words. She never quits."

"What do you know about this *hombre*, Polti?" asked Lance.

"Bert Polti? He's a sidewinder. Always has money, never does nothin'. He's plumb bad, an' plenty fast with that shootin' iron."

"He hangs out at the Spur?"

"Mostly. Him and them pards of his . . . Joe Daniels, Skimp Ellis, and Henry Bates. They're bad, all of them, and the bartender at the Spur is tough as a boot."

Lance started for the door. Rusty stared after him for an instant, then shrugged.

"Well," he said, "I'm buyin' a ticket. This is one ride I want to take." And he swung along after Lance

Lance walked up on the boardwalk and shoved open the batwing doors of the Spur. Bert Polti had been looking for trouble, and now Lance was. Slow to anger, it mounted in him now like a tide, the memory of those small, vicious eyes and the tenseness of the man as he stood, set to make a kill.

Never a troublemaker, Lance had always resented being bullied, nevertheless, and he resented seeing others pushed around. It was this, as much as a debt to pay, that had brought him to Botalla. There was as yet no tangible clue to what the trouble here was all about. He had only Steve Lord's version, one that seemingly ignored the rights of Mort Davis. Yet now Polti was buying in. Polti had deliberately tried to frame him with a killing. Lance hadn't a doubt but that Polti had planned to plant gold dust in his saddlebags.

III

A half dozen men were loitering about the bar when Lance walked in, turned, and looked around.

"Where's Polti?" he demanded.

One of the men he had seen talking to Polti was sitting at a table nearby, another stood at the bar.

There was no reply. "I said," Lance repeated sharply, "where's Polti?"

"You won't find out nothin' here, stranger," the seated man drawled, his tone insulting. "When Polti wants you, he'll get you."

Lance took a quick step toward him and, catching a flicker of triumph in the man's eye, wheeled to see an upraised bottle aimed at his head. Before the man who held it could throw, Lance's gun fairly leaped from its holster. It roared and the shot caught the bottle just as it left the man's hand.

Liquor flew in all directions, and the man sprang back, splattered by it.

Holstering his gun, Lance stepped in and caught the man by the shirt and jerked him around. Instantly the fellow swung. Turning him loose, Lance hooked a short left to the chin, then stabbed two fast jabs to the face. He feinted, and threw a high hard right. The fellow went down and rolled over on the floor.

Without a second's warning, Lance whirled around and grabbed the wrist of the man at the chair, spun him around, and hurled him to the floor.

"All right!" he snapped. "Talk, or take a beatin'! Where's Polti?"

"The devil with you!" Lance's latest victim snarled. "I'll kill you!"

Then Lance had him off the floor, slammed him against the bar, and proceeded to slap and backhand him seven times so fast the eye could scarcely follow. His grip was like iron, and before that strength the man against the bar felt impotent and helpless.

"Talk, cuss you!" Lance barked, and slapped him again. The man's head bobbed with the force of the blow. "I'm not talkin' for fun!" Lance said. "I want an answer!"

"Apple Cañon," the man muttered surlily, "and I hope he kills you."

Lance slammed him to the floor alongside the first man, then spun on his heel, and walked out. As he came through the door, he saw Rusty Gates standing outside, hand on his gun. Gates grinned.

"Didn't take long," he said dryly. "You operate pretty fast, pardner."

"Where's Apple Cañon?" Lance demanded.

"Well," Gates said, and rolled his quid of chewing in his jaws, "Apple Cañon is almost due south of here, down close to the border. That's where Nita Riordan hangs out."

"Who's she?" Lance wanted to know.

"Queen of the Border, they call her. Half Irish, half Mexican, and all dynamite. The best-looking woman in the Southwest, and a tiger when she gets started. But it ain't her you want to watch. It's Brigo. Jaime Brigo is a big Yaqui half-breed who can sling a gun as fast as the Brockmans, track like a bloodhound, and is loyal as a Saint Bernard. Also, he weighs about two pounds less than a ton of coal."

"What's the place like . . . a town?"

"No. A bar, a bunkhouse, and three or four houses. It's a hang-out for outlaws. And, feller, it ain't no place for a man t'go lookin' for Bert Polti. That's his bailiwick."

Lance saddled Buck, his buckskin, and headed south, leaving Rusty at the stable, staring thoughtfully after him. The day was beginning to fade now, and he could see the sun grow larger as it slid away toward the western mountains. There was still heat. It would not be tempered until after the sun was gone, until the long shadows came to make the plains cool.

The bunch grass levels were dotted with mesquite and clumps of prickly pear, and Lance rode on through them, letting the buckskin have his head on the narrow winding trail. Prairie dog towns were all about, but they disappeared as the rocks grew closer. Once he saw a rattler, and there were always buzzards, circling on slow, majestic wings above the waste below.

When he had gone no more than two miles, he left the trail and started cross-country, still thinking of Polti. He did not trust this man. He began to dig and pry in his memory, trying to uncover some clue as to Polti's actions. But more and more it became apparent that the secret of all the trouble lay in something he did not know.

The dim trail he had taken when he left the main trail to Apple Cañon was lifting now, skirting the low hills, steadily winding higher and higher. The story that he was going to Apple Cañon was a good one. It would cover up what he actually intended to do. And soon he would go to Apple Cañon.

Polti was dangerous. He knew that. Nor did he underrate the two men he had beaten up in the Spur. Their kind were coyotes who would follow a man for months for a chance to pull him down.

There was menace in this country, an impending

sense of danger that would not leave him. There was more here than met the eyes, more than the smile on tall, handsome Steve Lord's face, more than the sullen anger of the lovely, pampered Tana. There was death here, death and the acrid smell of gunpowder.

What did they know? What was behind the message he had received that had brought him here? Was it just another range war, or was it more?

Yet anyone who had lived in Texas through the Taylor and Sutton feud knew that range war could be deadly. And in Texas these days men rode with awareness. The wire was stirring up old feelings, old animosities. The big ranches were all stringing wire now. The smaller ranches were doing likewise. Starved for range for their herds, and pinched down to small areas, they saw extinction facing them if they did not fight. And they had neither the wealth to hire gunmen, nor the strength to fight without them unless they banded together.

Joe Wilkins, who Lance had learned was a nester, had been slain. The mention of his name and the quick surge of feeling had been enough to indicate that submerged fires burned here, and close to the surface. Any little spark might touch off an explosion that would light a thousand fires along the border, and turn it into an inferno of gunsmoke. Men were all carrying guns. They were carrying spare ammunition, too. They were ready, one and all. They rode the range, or rode fence with rifles across their saddle bows, and their keen eyes searched every clump of mesquite or prickly pear. Joe Wilkins had died, fences had been cut, and the ugly shape of war was lifting its head.

It was a time when men shot first and asked questions afterward. The notorious outlaw, Sam Bass, was riding the trails, robbing banks and trains. John Wesley Hardin was running up his score of twenty-seven men killed. King Fisher had 500 men riding to his orders on both sides of the border, King Fisher with his tiger-skin chaps and silver-loaded sombrero. Wild Bill Hickok, Bat Masterson, Billy Tilghman, Ben Thompson, and a hundred other gun slicks and toughs were riding the trails, acting as marshals in towns, or gambling.

The long fences were cutting down the range. The big ranches would still have range, but there would be too little grass for the cattle of the small ranchers. For them it was the end, or a battle for survival, and such a battle could have but one result. Yet the small ranchers were banding together. They were wearing guns.

From the crest of a ridge, Lance looked over the valley of Lost Creek and could see the long silvery strands of barbed wire stretching away as far as the eye could reach.

"I don't know, about this wire business," he mused, patting the buckskin on the shoulder. "I don't know who's right. There's arguments for both sides. It gives everybody a chance to improve breedin' and have crops, and anybody can see the longhorn is on the way out. Too little beef. These whitefaces now, they have something. They carry a lot more beef than a longhorn. You an' me, Buck, mebbe we're on the way out, too. We're free, and we go where we please, and we don't like fences. If they build fences, this country is finished for us. We'll have to go to Dakota, or mebbe to Mexico or the Argentine."

The buckskin turned down the little trail through the tumbled boulders and cedar, a dim, concealed little trail that the sure-footed mountain horse followed even in the vague light of late evening. This was not an honest man's trail, but Lance was not worried for he knew the manner of man he rode to see. That man who would never be less than honest, but he would fight to the last ditch for what he believed to be his own.

The trail dipped into a hollow several hundred yards across, and, when Lance had ridden halfway across it, he dismounted and led his horse into a sheltered position behind a boulder. It would be a long wait, for he was early. Sitting against a boulder, he watched the declining sun fall slowly westward, watched the shadows creep up the rocky walls, and the sunlight splash color upon the cliffs.

He must have fallen asleep, for when he awakened the stars were out, and he judged several hours must have passed.

It was quiet, yet when Lance lifted his eyes, it was in time to catch the gleam of starlight on a pistol barrel aimed over a rock. Then, even as he moved, the muzzle flowered with flame. As he hurled himself desperately to one side, he heard the bullet strike, then again, and something struck him a wicked blow on the back of the head. He tumbled on his face among the boulders. In his fading consciousness he seemed to feel something hot and sticky along his cheek. . . .

The first thing Lance knew, a long time later, was the throbbing pain in his skull as though a thousand tiny iron men were hammering with red-hot hammers at the shell of his skull, pounding and pounding. He opened his eyes to see a distant star shining through a crevice in the rocks across the hollow. Then he saw something long and dark lying upon the ground. It was like the body of a man.

Turning over painfully, Lance got his hands under him and pushed himself up to his knees. For a long time then he was still, and his head swayed and seemed like an enormous, uncontrollable thing. He forced his eyes to focus, but the starlight was too slight to help him to see more than he had.

Then he got a hand on the rock beside him, and pushed himself to his feet. There he remained, leaning against the rock. One hand dropped instinctively to his gun on the right side, then he felt for the other. Both were there.

The first shot, if there had been more than one, had missed him. It had either ricocheted off a rock then and hit him, or else the unseen killer had fired again.

He apparently had been left for dead. Feeling of his skull, he could understand why, for his hair was matted with blood.

Feeling around, his head throbbing fiercely, he found his hat and hung it around his neck by the rawhide chin strap. His head was too swollen for him to wear the sombrero. Stumbling to where he had left his horse, he found Buck waiting patiently. The yellow horse pricked up his ears and whinnied softly.

"Sorry, Buck," Lance whispered. "You should've been in the stable by now, with a good bait of oats."

He had swung into the saddle and turned down into the hollow before he remembered the shape on the ground. Then he saw it again.

There was more than the shape, for there was a standing horse. He dismounted and, gun in hand, walked cautiously over to the body. It was that of a stranger. In the vague starlight he could see only the outline of the man's features, but it was no one he knew. Then he saw the white of the envelope.

Stooping, his head pounding, he picked it up. There was writing on the back. By the light of a shielded match, he read a painful scrawl:

Mort needs help bad. I wuz dry-gulched. He koodnt kum.

It was written on the back of a letter addressed to Sam Carter, Lost Creek Ranch. Scratched by a dying man.

Thrusting the letter into his pocket, Lance wheeled his horse and rode away down the trail.

Lost Creek Ranch lay ahead and to the south, but he turned the buckskin again and rode away from the trail, skirting a cluster of rocks and heading for the ranch, whose position he had ascertained from Rusty, and knew from a map that had been sent him. He drew his rifle from its boot and put it across his saddle bow.

Still several miles away, he saw a glow in the sky. A glow of burning buildings. His eyes grew hard, and he spoke urgently to Buck. The long-geared yellow horse quickened his pace.

Lance passed what must have been Mort Davis's fence, but some of the posts were down, and the wire was gone. Lance refrained from watching the fire, keeping his eyes on the surrounding darkness. Maybe he was too late. A house was burning, and perhaps Mort Davis was dead. Suddenly he saw a man run out of the shadows.

"That you, Joe?" the man shouted.

Lance reined in, and swung his horse on an angle to the man. The fellow came closer.

"What's the matter?" he demanded. "Can't you hear me?"

The speaker was one of the two men Lance had whipped in the bar earlier that day. They recognized each other at the same instant. With a startled gasp the fellow went for his gun. Lance pulled the trigger without shifting the rifle, and the man grabbed his stomach, sliding from the saddle with a groan.

IV

Without looking down, Lance started toward the glow of the fire, his face set and angry. Had they killed Mort?

They had not. Lance was still several hundred yards away when he saw a rifle flash and heard the heavy bark of Mort's old Sharps. Several shots replied.

Touching spurs to the buckskin, Lance whipped into the circle near the flames at a dead run, snapping three quick shots into a group of men near a low adobe wall. It was a gamble at that speed, but the attacking group was bunched close. There was a cry of pain, and one of them whirled about. He was fully in the light and his chest loomed up. Lance put a shot into him as he flashed abreast of the man, heard a bullet whip past his own ear. Then he was gone into the darkness beyond the light of the flames.

Sliding from saddle, Lance put the rifle to his shoulder and shot twice. Reloading in haste, he began smoking up every bit of cover near the burning house, taking targets when they offered, and seeking the darkest spots of cover at other times. When his rifle was emptied, he dropped it to his side and opened up with a six-gun.

Men broke from cover and ran for their horses. The old Sharps bellowed in protest at their escape, and one of the men fell headlong. He scrambled up, but made only three steps before he pitched over again, dangerously near the flames.

Again Lance reloaded, then walked forward.

"Mort!" he called. "Come out of there, you old wolf! I know your shootin'!"

A tall, dark-bearded man in a battered black felt hat sauntered down from the circle of rocks at the foot of the cliff.

"Looks like you got here just in time, friend," he said. "You see Sam?"

Briefly Lance explained. Then he jerked his head in the direction the attackers had taken. "Who were they?" he asked.

"I don't know. Mebbe Webb Steele's boys. Him and Lord want me out of here, the worst way." He scratched the stubble on his lean jaws. "Let's have us a look."

Three men had been left behind. With the man Lance had killed out on the prairie, that made four. It had been a costly lesson. Well, Lance told himself, they should have known better than to tackle an old he-wolf like Mort Davis.

A lean, gangling sixteen-year-old strolled down from the rocks. He carried a duplicate of his father's Sharps. He stood beside his father and stared at the bodies.

"Don't look like nobody I ever seen," Mort said thoughtfully, "but Webb and Chet both been a-gettin' in some new hands."

"Pap," the youngster said, "I seen this one in Botalla trailin' with Bert Polti."

Lance studied the man's face. It wasn't one of the men he knew. "Mort," he asked, "where do the Brockmans figger in this?"

The old man puckered his brow. "The Brockmans? I didn't know they was in it. Abel Brockman rode for Steele once, but not no more. He got to sparkin' Tana, and the old man let him go. He didn't like it none, neither."

"It don't look right," Lance said as he rubbed his jaw reflectively. "Lord and Steele are supposed t'be fightin', but so far all I've seen is this gang that trails with Polti. They jumped me in town."

"Watch them Brockmans," Mort said seriously. "They're poison mean, and they never fight alone. Always the two of 'em together, and they got this gunfightin' as a team worked out mighty smooth. They always get you in a spot where you can't get the two to once."

Lance looked around. "Burned all your buildin's, didn't they? Any place you can live?"

"Uhn-huh. We got us a little cave back up here. We lived there before we built us a house. We'll make out. We're used to gettin' along without much. This here's the best place we had for a long time if we can keep it."

"You'll keep it," Lance promised, his face harsh and cold.

Mort Davis had done his share in making the West a place to live. He was getting old now, and deserved the rewards of his work. No big outfit, or outlaws either, was going to drive him off, if Lance could help it.

"Who knew this Sam Carter was to meet me?" he asked. "Or that you were?"

"Nobody I know of," said old Mort. "Carter's a 'puncher who started him a little herd over back of the butte. We worked together some. He was settin' for chuck when them riders come down on us. I asked him to get you."

Lance sketched the trouble in Botalla, then added the account of his run-in with Tana Steele. Mort grinned at that.

"I'd a give a purty to seen that," he said. "Tana's had her head for a long time. Drives that there buck-board like a crazy woman! At that, she can ride nigh anythin' that wears hair, and she will! Best lookin' woman around here, too, unless it's Nita Riordan."

"The woman at Apple Cañon?" Lance asked quickly.

"Yep. All woman, too. Runs that shebang by her-self. Almost, that is. Got her a Yaqui half-breed to help. Ain't nobody to fool with, that Injun."

"You better hole up and stay close to home, Mort," Lance said after a minute. "I'm dead tired, but I've some ridin' to do. I caught a couple of hours' sleep back in the hollow before the trouble."

He swung into saddle and started back over the trail. It was late and he was tired, but he needed more information before he could even start to figure things out. One thing he knew. He must talk to Lord and Steele and try to stop the trouble until they could get together. And he must get more information.

Four of the enemy had died, but even as he told himself that, he remembered that none of the dead men had been in any sense a key man. They were just straw men, men who carried guns and worked for hire, and more could be found to fill their places.

And then Sam Carter was gone. A good man, Sam. A man who could punch cows, and who had enough stuff in him to start his own place, and to fight for what he knew was right. No country could afford to lose men like that.

Suddenly, on the inspiration of the moment, Lance whirled the buckskin from the trail and headed for the Webb Steele spread. He could try talking to Steele, anyway.

He was well into the yard before a man stepped from the shadows.

"All right, stranger! Keep your hands steady. Now light, easy-like, and walk over here."

Lance obeyed without hesitation, carefully keeping his hands in front of him in the light from the ranch house window. A big man stepped from the shadows and walked up to him. Instinctively Lance liked the hard, rugged face of the other man.

"Who are you?" the man demanded.

"Name of Lance. Ridin' by and thought I'd drop in and have a talk with Webb Steele."

"Lance?" Something sparked in the man's eyes.

"You the gent had the run-in with Miss Tana?"

"That's me. She still sore?"

"Lance"—the older man chuckled—"shore as I'm Jim Weston, you've let yourself in for a packet of trouble. That gal never forgets! When she come in this afternoon, she was fit to be tied!" He holstered his gun. "What you aimin' to see Webb about?"

"Stoppin' this war. Ain't no sense to it."

"What's your dicker in this?" Weston asked shrewdly. "Man don't do nothin' unless he's got a angle somewheres."

"What's your job here, Weston?" Lance said.

"Foreman," Weston announced. "Why?"

"Well, what's the ranch makin' out of this war? What are you makin'?"

"Not a cussed thing, cowboy. She's keepin' me up nights, and we got all our 'punchers guardin' fence when they should be tendin' to cows. We're losin' cattle, losin' time, losin' wire, and losin' money."

"Shore. Well, you don't like that. I don't like it, either. But my own angle is Mort Davis. Mort's a friend of mine, and, Weston, Mort's goin' to keep his place in Lost Creek. He'll keep it, or, by glory, there'll be Lord and Steele 'punchers planted under every foot of it."

"Think you're pretty salty, don't you?" Weston demanded, but there was a glint of understanding in his eye. "Well, mebbe you are."

"I've been around, Weston. But that don't matter. You and me can talk. You're an old trail hand yourself.

140

You're a buffalo hunter, too. What you got against Mort?"

"Nothin'. He's a sight better hand and a whole lot better man than lots of 'em ridin' for this ranch now." He shook his head. "I know what you mean, mister. I know exactly. But I don't make the rules for the ranch. Webb does . . . Webb, or Tana."

They stepped inside the ranch house, and Weston tapped on an inner door. At a summons, he opened it. Big Webb Steele was tipped back in his chair across the table from the door. His shirt was open two buttons, showing a hairy chest, and his hard level eyes seemed to stare through and through Lance. To his right was Tana, and, as she saw Lance, she came to her feet instantly, her eyes blazing. Across the table was a tall, handsome man in a plain black suit of fine cut, a man with blue-gray eyes and a small, neatly trimmed blond mustache.

"You!" Tana burst out. "You have the nerve to come out here?"

"I reckon, ma'am," Lance drawled, and he smiled slyly. "I didn't reckon you carried your whip in the house. Or do you carry it everywhere?"

"You take a high hand with my daughter, Lance, if that's your name," Webb rumbled, glancing from Tana to Lance and back. "What happened between you two?"

"Steele," Lance said, grinning a little, "your daughter was drivin' plumb reckless, and we had a few words in which I attempted to explain that the roads wasn't all built for her own pleasure."

Webb chuckled. "Young feller, you got a nerve. But Tana can fight her own battles, so heaven have mercy on your soul."

"Well," Lance said, "you spoke of me takin' a high hand with your daughter. If my hand had been applied where it should have been, it might've done a lot more good."

Webb grinned again, and his hard eyes twinkled. "Son, I'd give a hundred head of cows to see the man as could do that. It'd be right interestin'."

"Father!" Tana protested. "This man insulted me."

"Ma'am," Lance interrupted, "I'd shore admire to continue this argument some other time. Right now I've come to see Mister Steele on business."

"What business?" Webb Steele demanded, cutting short Tana's impending outburst.

"War business. You're edgin' into a three-cornered war that's goin' to cost you plenty. It's goin' to cost Chet Lord plenty, too. I come to see about stoppin' it. I want to get a peace talk between you and Chet Lord an' Mort Davis."

"Mort Davis?" Webb exploded. "That no-account nester ain't goin' to make no peace talk with me! He'll get off that claim or we'll run him off!" Webb's eyes were blazing. "You tell that long-geared high-binder to take his stock and get!"

"He's caused a lot of trouble here," the man with the blond mustache said, "cutting fences and the like. He's a menace to the range." He looked up at Lance

"I'm Victor Bonham," he added. "Out from New York."

Lance had seated himself, and he studied Bonham for an instant, then looked back at Webb Steele, ignoring the Eastern man.

"Mister Steele," he said, "you've got the rep of bein' a square shooter. You come West with some durned good men, some of the real salty ones. Well, so did Mort Davis. Mort went farther West than you. He went on to Santa Fé and to Salt Lake. He helped open this country up. Then he finds him a piece of ground and settles down. What's so wrong about that?" Lance shifted his chair a little, then went on. "He fought Comanches and Apaches. He built him a place. He cleaned up that water hole. He did things in Lost Creek you'd never have done. You'd never have bothered about it but for this fencin' business. Well, Mort Davis moved in on that place, and he's a-goin' to stay. I, for one, mean to see he stays." He leaned forward. "Webb Steele, I ain't been hereabouts long, but I been here long enough to know something mighty funny is goin' on. Mort Davis was burned out tonight, by somebody's orders, an' I don't think the orders were yours or Chet Lord's, either. Well, as I said, Mort stays right where he is, and, if he dies, I'm goin' to move in an' bring war to these hills like nobody ever saw before."

"You talk mighty big for a loose-footed cowhand," Bonham said, smiling coldly. "We might decide not to let you leave here at all."

143

Lance turned his head slowly at the direct challenge and for a long minute he said nothing, letting his chill green eyes burn into the Easterner. "I don't know what your stake is in this, Bonham," he said evenly, "but when I want to leave here, I'm goin' to. I'll leave under my own power, and, if I have to walk over somebody in gettin' out, I could start with you."

"Better leave him alone, Bonham," a new voice interrupted. "He means what he says."

They all looked up, startled. Rusty Gates stood in the doorway, a sardonic smile on his hard red face.

"I was ridin' by," he explained, "and thought I'd rustle some coffee. But take a friendly tip."

Bonham laughed harshly. "I. . . ."

"Better shut up, New York man," Gates said. "There's been enough killin' tonight. You keep talkin', you're goin' to say the wrong thing." Rusty smiled suddenly, and glanced at Lance, his eyes twinkling. "Y'see"—he lighted his smoke—"I've heard Lance Kilkenny was right touchy about what folks said of him."

V

The name dropped into the room like a bombshell Tana's hands went to her throat, and her eyes widened. Webb Steele dropped his big hands to the table and his chair legs slammed down. Jim Weston backed up a little, his tongue wetting his lips.

It was Bonham, the man from New York, who

Lance Kilkenny was watching, and in Bonham's eyes he saw a sudden blaze of white, killing rage. The man's lips drew back in a thin line. If ever lust to kill was in a man's face, it was in Victor Bonham's then. An instant only, and then it was gone so suddenly that Kilkenny wondered if it had not been a hallucination.

"Did you say . . . Kilkenny?" Webb Steele demanded. "The gunfighter?"

"That's right." Lance's voice seemed to have changed suddenly. "My name is Lance Kilkenny. Mort Davis was in trouble, so I came to help him." He glanced up at Webb. "I don't want trouble, if I can avoid it, but they tried to burn out Mort and wipe him out."

"What happened?" Bonham demanded.

"Four men died," Lance said quietly. "They were not men anybody ever saw ridin' with Steele or Lord." He smiled a little. "Mort's still around, and still able."

Bonham was staring at him. "Yes, I seem to recall something about a man named Kilkenny being nursed by Davis, after a fight."

Lance got up. "Think it over, Mister Steele. I'm not ridin' for war. I never asked for trouble with any man. But Mort's my friend. Even with two old prairie wolves like you and Chet Lord there can be peace. You two should get together with Mort. You'd probably like each other."

Kilkenny stepped backward out of the door and went down the steps to the buckskin. Tana Steele stood there beside the horse. He had seen her slip from the room an instant before he left.

"So," she, said, scorn in her voice, "you're a gunman. I might have known it. A man who shoots down other men, less skilled than he, then holds himself up as a dangerous man."

"Ma'am," Kilkenny said quietly, taking the bridle "I've killed men. Most of 'em needed it, all of 'em asked for it. What you say doesn't help any, or make it worse." He swung into the saddle. "Ma'am," he added softly, "you're shore pretty in the moonlight . . . where a body can't see the meanness in you. You've either got an awful streak somewhere to make you come out here and say somethin' unpleasant, or else"—he grinned impudently—"you're fallin' in love with me."

Tana started back angrily. "In love with you? Why . . why, you conceited, contemptible. . . ."

But the buckskin swung around and Lance dropped an arm about her waist and swung her from the ground. He was laughing, and then he kissed her. He held her and kissed her until her lips responded almost in spite of themselves. Then he put her down and swung out of the ranch yard at a gallop, lifting his voice in song.

> *Old Joe Clark has got a cow*
> *She was muley born.*
> *It takes a jaybird forty-eight hours*
> *To fly from horn to horn.*

Tana Steele, shaking with anger or some other emotion less easily understood, stood staring after him. She was still staring when his voice died away in the distance.

Then she heard another horse start up, and watched it gallop down the trail after Lance Kilkenny.

It was several minutes before the rider caught up with Kilkenny, and found him, gun in hand, facing downtrail from the shadows at the edge. It was Rusty Gates. "What do you want?" Kilkenny demanded.

Rusty leaned forward and patted his black on the neck.

"Why, I reckon I want to ride along with you, Kilkenny. I hear you're a straight shooter, and I guess you're the only *hombre* I ever met up with could get into more trouble than me. If you can use a man to side you, I'd shore admire to ride along. I got an idea," he added, "that in days to come you can use some help."

"Let's ride, Rusty," Kilkenny said quietly. "It's getting late. . . ."

When Lance Kilkenny rolled out of his blankets in the early dawn, he glanced over at Gates. The redhead was still snoring. Kilkenny grinned, then shook his boots carefully to clear out any wandering tarantulas or scorpions that might have holed up for the night. Grimly he contemplated a hole in his sock. No time for that now. He pulled the sock down to cover the exposed toe, and slid the boot on. Then he got up. Carefully he checked his guns.

He moved quietly out of camp. For ten minutes he made a painstaking search of the area. When he returned to camp, he saddled his horse and rode quietly away. He was back, and had bacon frying when Rusty awakened and sat up.

They had camped on a cedar-covered mountainside with a wide view of Lost Creek Valley. From the ridge above they could see away into the purple distance of the mountains of Mexico. The air was brisk and cool with morning.

Coffee was bubbling in the pot when Rusty walked over.

"You get around, pardner," he said. "Shore, I slept like a log. Hey!" He looked startled and pleased. "You got bacon!"

"Got it last night from that Mexican where we got the *frijoles*. He's got him a half dozen hogs."

Rusty shook himself, and grinned. Then he looked up, suddenly serious.

"Ever see this *hombre* Bonham before?" he asked.

"No." Kilkenny glanced sideward at Gates. "Know him?"

"No. He ain't from around here."

"I wonder."

"You wonder? Why? They said he was from New York. He looks like a pilgrim."

"Yeah, he does." Lance poured coffee into two cups. "But he knew about Mort carin' for me after the fight with the Webers."

"Heard it around probably. I heard that myself." Rusty grinned. "You're too suspicious."

"I'm still alive." Lance Kilkenny grinned wryly.

Rusty nodded. "You got something there. Don't pay to miss no bets. Who you think Bonham is?"

Lance shrugged. "No idea."

"You had an idea last night. You said this fightin' wasn't all Lord an' Steele."

"You think it is?" asked Kilkenny.

Rusty shook his head. "No. Can't be. But who?"

"You been here longer than I have. How does she stack up to you? Who stands to gain but Steele and Lord? Who stands to gain if they both get gunned out or crippled?"

"Nobody. Them two have got it all, everywheres around here. Except for Mort, of course, but Mort ain't grabby. He wants his chunk of Lost Creek Valley, that's all."

"Rusty, you ever see a map of this country?"

"Map? Shucks, no! Don't reckon there is one. Who'd want a map?"

"Maps are handy things," Kilkenny said, sipping his coffee. "Sometimes a country looks a sight different on a map than you think it does. Sometimes, when you get a bird's eye view of things, you get a lot of ideas. Look here."

Drawing with his finger in the sand, Lance Kilkenny drew a roughly shaped V showing the low mountains and hills that girded the Live Oak country. Off to one side he drew in Lost Creek Valley.

"Right here, where it opens on the main valley," he said, "is where Lord and Steele's fence lines come together."

"That's right, plumb right," Rusty agreed. "That's what all the fuss is about. Who gets the valley?"

"But notice," Lance said, "this V-shaped valley that is half Steele's and half Lord's runs from the point of the V up to the wide cattle ranges of Texas. And up there are other cow outfits, bigger than even Lord's and Steele's. Fine stock, too. I come down through there a while back and rode over some fine range. Lots of whiteface bulls brought in up there. The stock is bein' improved. In a few years this is goin' to be one of the greatest stock-raisin' countries in the world. The fences won't make much difference at first except to limit the size of the roundups. There won't be no more four county roundups, but the stock will all improve, more beef per steer, and a bigger demand for it. The small ranchers can't afford to get good bulls. They'll cut fences here and there, as much to let bulls in with their old stock as anything. But that's only part of it. Look at all these broad miles of range. They'll be covered with fat stock, thousands upon thousands of head. It'll be fat stock, good grass and plenty of water. They'll shift the herds and feed the range off little by little. You've punched cows long enough to have rustled a few head. Huh, we all have now and again. Just think now, all this is stock country up here above the V. Now foller my finger."

He drew a trail in the dust down through the point of

the V into the country below. "See?" he asked.

Rusty furrowed his brow and spoke thoughtfully. "You mean somebody could rustle that stock into Mexico? Shore, but they'd have to drive rustled cows across the Steele and the Lord spreads, and. . . ." His eyes narrowed suddenly. "Say, pardner, I get it. You mean, if Lord and Steele was both out of it, whoever controlled that V could do as he danged well pleased down there. Right?"

Kilkenny nodded. "What's this place at the point of the V?"

"That's Apple Cañon. It's the key to the whole country, ain't it? And it's a hang-out for outlaws!"

"Shore, Apple Cañon. The Live Oak country is like a big funnel that will pour rustled stock down into Mexico, and whoever controls the Live Oak and Apple Cañon controls rustlin' in all this section of Texas!"

"Well, I'll be durned!" Rusty spat into the dust. "And that's where Nita Riordan lives!"

Kilkenny got up. "That's right, Rusty. Right as rain, and we're ridin' to have a little talk with Nita. We're ridin' now."

Llano Trail lifted up over the low hills from the Live Oak country and headed down again through Forgotten Pass, winding leisurely across the cactus-studded desert where only the coyotes prowled and rattlesnakes huddled in the shade of boulders, and the chaparral cock ran along the dim trails. Ahead of the two horsemen, lost like motes in a beam in all the vast emptiness of the desert, could be seen the great, ragged rocks of the mountains. Not mountains of great height, but huge, upthrust masses of rock, weirdly shaped as though wrought by some insane god.

It was a country almost without water, yet a country where a knowing man might live, for barrel cactus, the desert reservoir, grew there. One might cut a hole in the cactus and during the night or in a matter of an hour or so considerable liquid, cool and fresh, would gather. Always sufficient for life.

The buckskin ambled easily, accustomed to long trails, and accustomed to having his head in pacing over the great distances. His was a long-stepping, untiring walk that ate up the miles.

The sun lifted from behind a morning cloud, and started climbing toward noon. Buzzards wheeled lazily, their far-seeing eyes searching the desert in an endless quest for food.

Slouching in his saddle, his hard face burned almost as red as his hair, Rusty Gates watched the rider ahead of him. It was easy to admire a fighting man, he thought. Always a fighter himself, Rusty fought because it was easy for him, because it was natural. He had punched cows, ridden the cattle trails north. He had, one time and another, tried everything, been everywhere a man could go on a horse. Usually he rode alone. But slowly and surely down the years he began picking up lore on Lance Kilkenny. He had it at his fingertips now.

VI

Everyone, Rusty Gates thought, knew about Hickok; everyone knew about John Wesley Hardin, and about Ben Thompson and his partner, Phil Coe. Not many knew about Kilkenny. He was a man who always moved on. He stayed nowhere long enough to build a solid reputation. Always it seemed, he had just gone. There was something so elusive about him, he had come to seem almost a phantom. Someone picked trouble with him, someone was killed, and Kilkenny was gone. Once they tried to rob him in a gambling den in Abilene. Two men had died. Apaches had cornered him in a ruined house in New Mexico, and, when the Apaches had drawn off, they had left seven dead behind them. In a hand-to-hand fight in Trail City he had whipped three men with fists and chairs. Then, when morning came, he was gone.

The stories of the number of men he had killed varied. Some said he had killed eighteen men, not counting Indians and Mexicans. The cattle buyer back in Dodge, who had made a study of such things, said he had killed not less than twenty-nine. Of this Kilkenny said nothing, and no man could find him to put the question.

"You know," Rusty said suddenly, breaking in on his own thoughts of Kilkenny, "the Brockmans hang out in Apple Cañon."

"Yeah." Kilkenny sat sideward in the saddle, to rest. "I know. We might run into 'em."

"Well," Rusty said, and he rolled the chew of tobacco in his jaws and spat, "there's better places to meet 'em than Apple Cañon. There'll be fifty men there, mebbe a hundred, and all friends of the Brockmans."

Kilkenny nodded and rolled a smoke. Then he grinned whimsically. "What you worried about?" he asked. "You got fifty rounds, ain't you?"

"Fifty rounds?" Gates exclaimed. "Shore, but shucks, man, I miss once in a while." He looked at Kilkenny speculatively. "You seen the Brockmans? They'll weigh about forty pounds more'n you, and you must weigh two hundred. I seen Cain Brockman shoot a crow on the wing!"

"Did the crow have a gun?" drawled Kilkenny.

That, decided Rusty, was a good question. It was one thing to shoot at a target even such a fleeting one as a bird on the wing. It was quite something else when you had to shoot at a man with a flaming gun in his fist. Yes, it made a sight of difference.

"By the way"—Kilkenny turned back in his saddle—"I want the Brockmans myself."

"Both of 'em?" Rusty was incredulous. "Listen, I. . . ."

"Both of 'em," Kilkenny said positively. "You keep the sidewinders off my back."

Rusty glanced up and saw a distant horseman coming toward them at an easy lope. He was still some distance away.

"Somebody comin'," he told Kilkenny. "One man."

"It's Steve Lord," Kilkenny said. "I picked him up a couple of miles back."

"Don't tell me you can see his face from here!" Rusty protested. "Why I can barely see it's a man!"

"Uhn-huh." Kilkenny grinned. "Look close. See the sunlight glintin' on that sombrero? Steve has a hatband made of polished silver disks. Not common."

Rusty spat. Easy enough when you figure it out, he thought, but not many would think of it. Now that it was mentioned he recalled that hatband. He had seen it so many times it no longer made an impression.

Suddenly he asked Kilkenny: "About that Mendoza deal. I was in Sonora after you killed him. I heard he was the fastest man in the world with a gun, then you beat him to it. Did you get the jump or was you just naturally faster?"

Kilkenny shrugged. "Didn't amount to much. He beat me to the draw, though."

"I didn't think anybody ever beat you," observed Rusty.

"He did. Mebbe he saw me a split second sooner. Fact, I think he did."

"How come he didn't kill you?" Rusty glanced at him curiously.

"He made a mistake." Kilkenny wiped sweat from Buck's neck. "He missed his first shot. Never," he added dryly, "miss the first one. You may not get another."

Steve Lord came up at a gallop and reined in

sharply. "You!" he said, as he glanced sharply from one to the other. "Didn't know you was interested down thisaway."

"Takin' a look at Apple Cañon," Rusty said. He grinned widely. "I'm a goin' to interduce Kilkenny to Nita."

"I heard you was Kilkenny," Steve said, and looked at him curiously. "I've talked to five men before who claimed to know you. Each gave a different description."

"Steve," Lance said, "this fight ain't goin' to do you or your old man any good. I had a talk with Webb Steele. I think we need a meetin' between your dad, Webb Steele, and Mort Davis to iron this trouble out."

"Mort Davis?" Steve exploded. "Why, Dad's threatened to shoot him on sight. They'd never dare get in the same room."

"I'll be there," Kilkenny said dryly. "If any shootin's done, I'll do it."

Steve shook his head doubtfully. "I'll talk to him, but it won't do any good. He's too hard-headed."

"So's Webb Steele," Rusty agreed, "but we'll bring him around."

"No need for anybody to fight," Kilkenny said. "I came in this to help Mort. You and your dad stand to lose plenty if this war breaks wide open. Why fight when it's to somebody else's interest?"

Steve's head jerked around. "What you mean by that?" he demanded.

Kilkenny looked up mildly, then drew deeply on his

cigarette, and flicked off the ash before he replied. "Because there's somebody else in this," he said then. "Somebody who wants Lord and Steele out of the way, somebody who stands to win a heap. Find out who that is, and we'll know the reason for range war."

Steve's face sharpened. He wheeled his horse. "You won't find anybody at Apple Cañon!" he shouted. "I saw the Brockman there!" Then he was gone.

"Scared," Rusty Gates suggested. "Scared silly."

"No," Kilkenny said, "he ain't scared. It's somethin' else."

Yet, as he rode on, he was not thinking of that, or of anything that had to do with this trouble except in the most remote way. He was thinking of himself, something he rarely allowed himself to do beyond caring for the few essential comforts of living, the obtaining of food and shelter. He was thinking of what lay ahead, for in his own mind he could see it all with bitter clarity.

This was an old story, and a familiar one. The West knew it, and would know it again and again in the bitter years to come. Struggle was the law of growth, and the West was growing up the hard way. It was growing up through a fog of gunsmoke, and through the acrid odor of gunpowder, and the sickly sweet smell of blood. Men would die, good men and bad, but strong men all, and a country needed its strong men. Such a country as this needed them doubly bad. Whether it would be today he did not know, but he knew there must be a six-gun showdown, and he had seen too many of them. He was tired. Young in years, he had ridden long on the out trail, and knew only too well what this meant. If he should be the best man, he would live to run again and to drift to a new land where he was not known as a killer, as a gunman. For a few days, a few months all would go well. Then there would come a time, as it was coming now, when it was freedom and right, or a fight to the death. Sometimes he wondered if it were worth it.

There was something familiar about this ride. He remembered it all so well. Ahead of him lay trouble, and going to Apple Cañon was typical of him, just what he would do. It was always his method to go right to the heart of trouble, and Apple Cañon seemed to be the key point here.

There was so much ahead. He did not underrate Bert Polti. The snake-eyed gunman was dangerous, quick as a cat, and vicious as a weasel. The man would kill and kill until he was finally put down full of lead. He would not quit, for there wasn't a yellow thing about the man. He would kill from ambush, yes. He would take every advantage, for he did not kill from bravado or for a reputation. He killed to gain his own ends, and for that reason there would be no limit to his killing. Yet at best Polti was a tool. A keen-edged tool, but a tool nevertheless. He was a gunman, ready to be used by a keener brain, and such a brain was using him now. Who it was, Kilkenny could not guess. Somehow he could not convince himself that behind the bluff boldness of Webb Steele lived the ice-cold mind of a killer. Nor from what he could discover was Chet Lord different.

No, the unknown man was someone else, someone beyond the pale of the known, someone relentless and ruthless, someone with intelligence, skill, and command of men. And afterward there would be only the scant food, the harsh living of the fugitive, then again a new attempt to find peace in new surroundings. Someday he might succeed, but in his heart he doubted it.

He was in danger. The thought impressed him little, for he had always been in danger. The man he sought this time would be aware by now that he knew the danger lay not in Steele or Lord, but outside of them. Yet his very action in telling them what he thought might force the unknown into the open. And that was what he must do. He must force the play until at every move it brought the unknown more and more into the open until he was compelled to reveal himself.

The direct attack. It was always best with the adroit man. Such a man could plan for almost anything but continuous frontal attack. And he, Kilkenny, had broken such plots before. But could he break this one? Looking over the field, he realized suddenly that he was not sure. This man was cool, deadly, and dangerous. He would anticipate Kilkenny's moves, and from the shelter of his ghost-like existence he could hunt him, pin him down, and kill him—if he was lucky.

Kilkenny looked curiously at the mountains ahead. Somewhere up there Forgotten Pass went over the mountains and then down to the Río Grande. It wasn't much of a pass, as passes go, and the section was barren, remote. But it would undoubtedly be an easy route over which to take cattle to Mexico, and many of the big ranches down there were buying, often planning to sell the rustled cattle they bought back across the border.

It was almost mid-afternoon before the two riders rounded the shoulder of rock and reined in, looking down the main street of the rickety little town of Apple Cañon. Kilkenny halted his horse and studied the situation. There were four clapboard buildings on one side of the street, three on the other.

"The nearest one is the sawbones," Rusty explained. "He's a renegade from somewheres, but a good doc. Next is the livery stable and blacksmith shop all in one. The long building next door is the bunkhouse. Forty men can sleep there, and usually do. The place after that is Bert Polti's. He lives there with Joe Deagan and Tom Murrow. On the right side the nearest building is Bill Sadler's place. Bill is a gambler. Did a couple of stretches for forgery, too, they say. He cooks up any kind of docyments you want. After his place is the big joint of Apple Cañon, the Border Bar. That's Nita's place. She runs it herself. The last house, the one with the flowers around, is Nita's. They say no man ever entered the place. You see"—Rusty glanced at Lance—"Nita's straight, hough there's been some has doubted it from time to ime. But Nita, she puts 'em right."

"And the place up on the cliffs beyond the town?" Kilkenny wondered. "Who lives there?"

"Huh?" Rusty scowled his puzzlement. "Where you mean?"

Kilkenny pointed. High on a rocky cliff, in a place hat seemed to be secure from all but the circling eagles, he could dimly perceive the outline of some sort of a structure. Even in the bright light, with the sun falling fully on the cliff, it was but a vague suggestion. Yet, even as he looked, he caught a flash of ight reflecting from something.

"Whoever lives there is a careful man," Kilkenny said dryly. "He's lookin' us over with a glass!"

Rusty was disgusted. "Well, I'll be hanged! I been here three times before, and once stayed five days, and never knowed that place was there."

Kilkenny nodded understandingly. "I'll bet a pretty you can't see it from the town. I just wonder who it is who's so careful? Who wants to know who comes to Apple Cañon? Who can hide up there and remain unknown?"

"You think . . . ?"

"I don't think anything . . . yet. But I mean to find out, some way. I'm a curious *hombre*, Gates."

VII

Kilkenny was in the lead by a dozen paces as the two
rode slowly down the street. A man sitting before the
Border Bar turned his head and said something
through the window, but aside from that there was no
movement.

Yet Kilkenny saw a man with a rifle in some rocks
at the end of the street, and there was a man with a
rifle in the blacksmith shop. The town, he thought
grimly, was well guarded.

They walked their horses to the hitching rail and
dismounted. The man sitting on the porch looked at
them curiously and spat off the end of the porch. His
eyes dropped to Kilkenny's tied-down guns, then
strayed to his face. His attention seemed to sharpen
and for an instant his eyes wavered to Rusty.

They stepped up on the porch and Kilkenny pushed
through the batwing doors. Rusty loitered on the
porch, brushing dust from his clothes.

"Travelin's dry business," he muttered.

"Risky, too," the watcher replied softly. "You're
askin' for trouble comin' here with him. The word's
out."

"For me, too, then," Rusty said. "We're riding
together."

"Like that, huh? Can't help you none, cowboy."

"Ain't askin'. Just keep out of the way."

Rusty stepped inside. Kilkenny was standing at the

bar. The bartender was leaning or the bar farther down, doing nothing. He was pointedly ignoring them.

As Rusty stepped through the doors, he heard Kilkenny say in a deceptively mild voice:

"I'd like a drink."

The bartender did not move a muscle, and gave no evidence that he heard.

"I'd like a drink," Kilkenny said, and his voice was louder.

The three men sitting in the room were covertly watching. Two of them sat against the west and south walls. The third man was across the room, almost behind Kilkenny, and against the east wall. The bar itself covered most of the north wall except where a door opened at one end. It apparently led to a back room.

"I'm askin' once more," Kilkenny said. "I'd like a drink."

The burly bartender turned toward him then, and his stare was hard, ugly.

"I don't hear you, stranger," he said insultingly. "I don't hear you, and I don't know you."

What happened then was to make legend in the border country. Kilkenny turned and his hand shot out. It grasped the bartender's shirt collar, and jerked—so hard that the bartender slid over the bar and crashed on the floor outside of it.

He hit the floor all sprawled out, then came up with a choking cry of anger. But Kilkenny was ready for him. A sharp left lanced at the bartender's eye, and a wicked right hook in the ribs made his mouth drop open. Then Kilkenny stepped in with a series of smashing, bone-crushing punches that pulped the big man's face and made him stagger back, desperately trying to protect his face with crossed arms. But Kilkenny was remorseless. He whipped a right to the midsection to bring the bigger man's arms down, then hooked a left to the chin that dropped the bartender to all fours.

Stopping quickly, Kilkenny picked the man up and smashed a looping right to the chin. The bartender staggered back across the room and hit the floor in a heap against the far wall.

It was over so suddenly, and Big Ed Gardner, the barkeep, was whipped so quickly and thoroughly that it left the astonished gunmen present staring. Before they could get set for it, Kilkenny sprang back.

"All right!" Kilkenny's voice cracked like a whip in the dead silence of the room. "If you want Kilkenny, turn loose your dogs!"

The name rang like a challenge in the room, and the three men started. The gunman against the west wall touched his lips with a nervous tongue. In his own mind he was sure of one thing. If they went through with their plan he himself was going to die. No one had told them the man they were facing was Kilkenny.

It caught them flat-footed. They sat deathly still

their faces stiff. Then, slowly, the man against the south wall began letting his hand creep away from his guns.

"All right, then," Kilkenny said evenly. "What was you to do here? Gun me down?"

Nobody spoke, and suddenly Kilkenny's gun was in his hand. How it got there no man could say. There was no flicker in his eyes, no dropping of his shoulder, but suddenly his hand was full, and they were looking down the barrel of the .45.

"Talk," Kilkenny said. "You, against the west wall. Tell me who sent you here, and what you was to do. Tell me, or I start shootin' your ears!"

The man swallowed, then wet his lips. "We wasn't to kill you," he said hoarsely. "We was to make you a prisoner."

Kilkenny smiled then. "All right. Mexico's south of here. Travel!"

The three men hit the door in a lump, struggled madly, then all three got out, swung onto their horses, and hit the road on a run.

A rifle cracked outside. Kilkenny stiffened, and stared at Rusty. It rang out twice more. Two neat, evenly spaced shots!

Kilkenny stepped quickly to a place beside the window. One of the fleeing gunmen had been shot down near the end of the street. The others, at almost equal distances, lay beyond.

"Who done that?" Rusty questioned.

"Evidently the boss don't like failure," Kilkenny

suggested, thin-lipped. He shrugged. "Well, I still want a drink. Guess I'll have to pour it myself."

"It won't be necessary," said a smooth feminine voice.

Both men turned, startled.

A girl stood at the end of the bar, facing them. She stood erect, her chin lifted a little, one hand resting on the bar. Her skin was the color of old ivory, her hair jet black and gathered in a loose knot at the nape of her neck. But it was her eyes that were most noticeable—and her mouth. Her eyes were hazel, with tiny flecks of a darker color, and they were large, and her lashes were long. Her lips were full, but beautiful, and there was a certain wistfulness in her face, a strange elusive charm that prevented the lips from being sensual. Her figure would have wrung a gasp from a marble statue, for it was seductively curved, and, when she moved, it was with a sinuous grace that had no trace of affectation.

She came forward, and Kilkenny found himself looking into the most amazingly beautiful eyes he had ever seen.

"I am Nita Riordan," she said. "Could I pour you a drink?"

Kilkenny's expression did not change. "Nita Riordan," he said quietly, "you could."

She poured two drinks and handed one to each of them. She did not glance at Big Ed who was beginning to stir on the floor.

"It seems you have had trouble," she said.

"A little . . . hardly worth mentionin'," Kilkenny said with a shrug. "Not so much trouble as any man would cheerfully go through to meet a girl like you."

"You are gallant, *señor*," Nita said, looking directly into his eyes. "Gallantry is always pleasant, and especially so here, where one finds it so seldom."

"Yes," Kilkenny said quietly, "and I am only gallant when I am sincere."

She looked at him quickly, as though anxious to find something in his face. Then she looked away quickly. "Sincerity is difficult to find in the Live Oak, *señor*," she said. "It has little value here."

"It still has value to some," he said, letting his eyes meet hers. "It has to me." He looked down at Big Ed. "I don't like to fight," he said slowly, "but sometimes it is necessary."

Her eyes flashed. "That is not sincere, *señor!*" she retorted severely. "No man who did not like to fight could have done *that!*" With a gesture she indicated Big Ed's face. "Perhaps it is that you like to fight, but do not like *having* to fight. There is a difference."

"Yes." He hitched his guns a little, swallowed his whiskey at a gulp, and looked back at her. "Nita Riordan," he asked quietly, "who is the man in the cliff house above Apple Cañon?"

Her eyes widened a little, then her face set in hard lines. He saw her lips part a little, and saw her quick breath.

"I cannot answer that, *señor*," she said. "If there is a man there, he would resent it. You saw what happened to three who failed? I would not like to die *señor*. There is much joy in living, even here where there are only outlaws and thieves. Even here the world can be bright, *señor*. For a cause, I can die. For nothing, no. To tell you now would be for nothing."

"They told me you were the boss at Apple Cañon," Kilkenny suggested.

"Perhaps. Things are not always what they seem *señor*."

"Then I'll go talk to the man on the cliff," Kilkenny said. "I'll ask him what he wants with Kilkenny, and why he prefers me alive rather than dead."

"Kilkenny?" Nita's eyes widened, and she stepped closer, her eyes searching his face. "You?"

"Yes. Are you surprised?"

She looked up at him, her eyes wide and searching. "I heard long ago, Kilkenny, that you were a good man. I heard that your guns spoke only when the need was great."

"I've tried to keep it that way."

"And you ride alone, Kilkenny?"

"I do."

"And are you never lonely, *señor*? For me, I have found it sometimes lonely."

He looked at her, and suddenly something in his eyes seemed to touch her with fire. He saw her eyes widen a little, and her lips part as though in wonderment. Kilkenny took a half step forward, and she seemed to lean to meet him. Then he stopped abruptly, and turned quickly, almost roughly away.

168

"Yes," he said somberly, "it has been lonely. It will be more so, now."

He turned abruptly toward the door and had taken three strides when her voice caught him.

"No! Not now to the cliff, *señor*. The time is not now. There will be many guns. Trust me, *señor*, for there will be another time." She stepped closer to him. "That one will be enough for you, *señor*, without others. He is a tiger, a fiend. Perdition knows no viciousness such as his, and he hates you. Why, I do not know, but he hates you with a vindictive hatred, and he will not rest until he kills you. Go now, and quickly. He will not shoot you if you ride away. He wants to face you, *señor*. Why, I do not know."

Kilkenny stopped and turned toward her, his green eyes soft, and strangely warm.

"Nita," he said softly, "I will ride away. He may be the man you love. Mebbe you're protectin' him, yet I don't believe either of them things. I'll trust you, Nita. It might be said that a man who trusts a woman is one who writes his name upon water, but I'll take the chance."

He stepped quickly from the door and walked to the buckskin. Gates, only a step behind, also swung into saddle. They rode out of town at a rapid trot.

"Whew!" Rusty Gates stared at Kilkenny. "Mister, when you try, you shore get results. I never saw Nita Riordan like she was today. Every man along the border's had ideas about her. She's hosswhipped a couple, knifed one, and Brigo killed a couple. But

169

today I'd 'a' swore she was goin' t'walk right into your arms."

Kilkenny shrugged. "Never put too much weight on a woman's emotions, Rusty. They ain't reliable. . . ."

Behind them, in the saloon at Apple Cañon, a door slowly opened. The man who stood in the door looking at Big Ed was even larger than the bartender. He seemed to fill the open door, seemed huge, almost too big to be human. Yet there was nothing malformed about him. He was big, but powerfully, splendidly built, and his Indian face was dark and strangely handsome. He moved down the bar with no more noise than a sliding of wind along the floor, and stopped close to Big Ed.

The bartender turned his battered, bloody face toward him.

"No," Brigo said softly, "you will not betray the *señorita*." His black eyes were dark with intent as he stared into Big Ed's. "If one word of this reaches *him*, I kill you! And when I kill you, *amigo mío*, it will not be nice, the way I kill."

"I ain't talkin'," Big Ed said gruffly through battered lips. "I had enough."

VIII

Nita was standing in her garden, one hand idly fingering a rose, when Brigo came through the hedge. He looked at her, and his lips parted over perfect teeth.

"You have found him, *señorita*," he murmured. "I see that. You have found this man for whom you waited."

She turned quickly. "Yes, Jaime. It is he. But has he found me?"

"Did you not see his face? His eyes? *Sí, señorita*, Jaime think he find you, too. He is a strong man, that one. Perhaps"—he canted his head speculatively— "so strong as Jaime."

"But what of *him?*" Nita protested. "He will kill him. He hates him."

"*Sí*, he hates. But he will not kill. I think now something new has come. This man, this Kilkenny. He is not the same." Brigo nodded thoughtfully. "I think soon, *señorita*, I return to my home. . . ."

Trailing a few yards behind Kilkenny, Rusty Gates stared up at the wall of the valley. A ragged, pine-spread slope fell away to a rocky cliff, and the sandy wash that ran at the base of it. It was a wild, lonely country. Thinking back over what he knew of this country, he began to see that what Kilkenny had said was the truth. Someone had planned to engineer the biggest rustling plot in Western history.

With this Live Oak country under one brand, cattle could be eased across its range and poured down through the mouth of the funnel into Mexico. By weeding the bigger herds carefully, they might bleed them for years without anyone finding out what was happening. On ranges where cattle were numbered in thousands, a few head from each ranch would not be missed, but in the aggregate it would be an enormous number. This was not the plan of a moment. It was no cowpuncher needing a few extra dollars for a blow-out. This was a steal on the grand scale. It was the design of a man with a brain, and with ruthless courage. Remembering the three men dead back at Apple Cañon, Rusty could see even more. The boss, whoever he was, would kill without hesitation, and on any scale.

Kilkenny was doing some thinking, too. The leader, whoever he was, was a man who knew him. Slowly and carefully he began to sift his past, trying to recall who it might be. Dale Shafter? No, Shafter was dead. He had been killed in the Sutton-Taylor feud. Anyway, he wasn't big enough for this. Card Benton? Too small. A small-time rustler and gambler. One by one he sifted their names, and man after man cropped up in his mind, men who had never rustled, men who were gamblers and gunslingers, men who had cold nerve and who were killers. But somehow none of them seemed to be the type he wanted. And who had fired at him that night in the hollow as he waited for Mort Davis? Who had killed Sam Carter? Was it the same man? Was he the leader? Kilkenny doubted it. This man wanted him alive, and that one had tried to kill him. Indeed, the man had left him for dead. Someone, too, had killed Joe Wilkins. That would take some looking into.

Kilkenny walked his horse down a weathered slide

and crossed a wash. The trail led through a low place walled on each side by low, sandy hills, covered with mesquite, bunch grass, and occasional prickly pear. This job of saving Davis's place for him was turning into something bigger than Lance Kilkenny had dreamed. It was becoming one of the biggest things he had ever walked into. One thing, at least—he had proved to himself that Steele and Lord were out of it. Now if he could bring them to peace with Mort Davis, the only thing left would be to fight it out with the mysterious boss of the gang.

Somehow, more and more, he was beginning to feel that there was more behind this plan than he imagined. This didn't seem like even a simple rustling scheme. Try as he might, he couldn't fit any man into it who he knew. Nor any he had heard of. Yet the fact remained that the leader knew him. Gun experts were as much a part of the West as Indians or cows. It was not an accident that there were so many. And they were, good and bad, essential to the making of the West. Kilkenny was one of the few who saw his own place in the scheme of things clearly. He knew just exactly what he meant, what he was.

Billy the Kid, Pat Garrett, Wes Hardin, Hickok, Ben Thompson, Tom Smith, Earp, Masterson, Tilghman, John Selman, and all the rest were a phase. Most of them cleared out badmen, opened up the West. They fought Indians and they were the rough, outer bark of the pioneering movement. The West was a raw country, and raw men came to it, but there had to be peace. These men, lawless as many of them were, were also an evidence of the coming of law and order, for many of them became sheriffs or marshals, became men who made the West safer to live in.

There could be an end to strife. It was not necessary to go on killing. It could be controlled, and one way to control it was to put the law in the hands of a strong man. Often he was himself a badman, and sometimes he killed the wrong man. But by and large, he kept many other gunmen from killing many more men, and brought some measure of order to the West. Yet this new outlaw leader, this mysterious man upon the cliff, this man who seemed to be pulling the strings from behind the scenes was not one of these. He was different, strange.

Shadows grew longer as the sun sank behind the painted hills, and a light breeze came from the south, blowing up from Mexico. There was a faint smell of dust in the air. Kilkenny glanced at Gates.

"Somebody fogged it along this trail not so long ago," he said. "Somebody who wanted to get some place in a hurry."

"Yeah." Rusty nodded. "And that don't mean anything good for us."

"Whoever the big mogul in this game is," Kilkenny said thoughtfully, "will try to break the trouble between Steele and Lord without delay."

"The worst of it is we don't know what he'll do, or where he'll strike next," Gates said.

They were riding at a steady trot toward Botalla when they saw a rider winging it toward them. Rusty flagged him down.

"Hey, what's the rush?" he demanded.

"All tarnation's busted loose!" the rider shouted excitedly. "Lord's hay was set afire, and Steele's fence cut. Some of Lord's boys had a runnin' fight with two of Steele's men, and in town there have been two gunfights!"

"Anybody killed?" Kilkenny demanded anxiously.

"Not yet. Two men wounded on Steele's side!" The cowboy put spurs to his horse and raced off into the night toward the Steele Ranch.

"Well, there goes your cattle war!" Rusty said. "This'll make Lincoln County look like nothin' at all! What do we do now?"

"Stop it, that's what."

Kilkenny whipped the buckskin around and in a minute they were racing down the road toward Botalla.

The main street was empty and as still as death, when they dashed up, but there were lights in the spur, and more lights in the bigger Trail House. Kilkenny swung down, loosened his guns in their holsters, and walked through the batwing doors of the Trail House.

Men turned quickly at his approach, and their voices died down. He glanced from one to the other, and his eyes narrowed.

"Any Steele men here?" he demanded. Two men

stepped forward, staring at him, hesitant, but ready for anything.

"We're from Steele's," he said. "What about it?"

"There'll be no war," Kilkenny said flatly. "Neither of you men is firin' a shot at a Lord man tonight. You hear?"

The nearest cowpuncher, a hard-bitten man with a scarred face, grinned, showing broken yellow teeth. "You mean, if I get shot at, I don't fight back? Don't be foolish, *hombre!* If I feel like fightin', I'll fight. Nobody tells me what to do."

Kilkenny's eyes narrowed. "I'm tellin' you." His voice cracked like a whip. "If you shoot, better get me first. If not, I'm comin' after you."

The man's face paled. "Then you talk to them Lord men," he persisted stubbornly, backing off a little. "I ain't anxious for no gunslingin'!"

Kilkenny wheeled and crossed to the Spur. Shoving the doors open, he stepped in and issued the same ultimatum to the Lord men. Several of them appeared relieved. But one man got up and walked slowly down the room toward Kilkenny.

Lance saw it coming. He stood still, watching the man come closer and closer. He knew the type. This man was fairly good with a gun but he wanted a reputation like Kilkenny's, and figured this was the time to get it. Yet there was a lack of certainty in the man's mind. He was coming, but he wasn't sure. Kilkenny was. No man had ever outshot him. He had the confidence given him by many victories.

"I reckon, Kilkenny," the Lord cowpuncher said, "it's time somebody called you. I'm shootin' who I want to, and I ain't takin' orders from you. I hear you're fast. Well, fill your hand!"

He dropped into a gunman's crouch, then froze and his mouth dropped open. He gulped, then swallowed. The gun in Kilkenny's hand was leveled at the pit of his stomach.

Somehow, in the gunfights he'd had before, it had never happened like that. There had been a moment of tenseness, then both had gone for their guns. But this had happened so suddenly. He had expected nothing like that heavy .45 aimed at his stomach, with the tall, green-eyed man standing behind it.

It came to him abruptly that all he had to do to die was drop his hand. All at once, he didn't want to die. He decided that being a gun slick wasn't any part of his business. After all, he was a cowpuncher.

Slowly, step by step, he backed up. Then he swallowed again. "Mister," he said, "I reckon I ain't the *hombre* I thought I was. I don't think there'll be any trouble with the Steele boys tonight."

Kilkenny nodded. "No need for trouble," he said quietly. "There's too much on this range, anyway."

He spun on his heel and walked from the barroom.

For an instant all was still, then the big cowpuncher looked around, and shook his head in amazement.

"Did you see him drag that iron?" he asked pleadingly. "Where the devil did he get it from? I looked, and there it was!"

177

There was silence for a long time, then one man said sincerely: "I heerd he was gun swift, but nothin' like that. Men, that's Kilkenny!"

Rusty Gates grabbed Kilkenny as he left the Spur.

"Kilkenny," he said, "there's a stranger rode in today. He asked for you. Got somethin' to tell you, he says. Hails from El Paso!"

"El Paso?" Kilkenny scowled. "Who could want to see me from there?"

Gates shrugged. "Purty well lickered, I hear." He lighted a smoke. "But he ain't talkin' fight. Just insists on seein' you."

"Where is he now?"

Kilkenny was thoughtful. El Paso. He hadn't been in El Paso since the Weber fight. Who could want to see him from there?

"He was at the Trail House," Gates said. "Come in just after you took off. Tall, rangy feller. Looks like a cowhand, all right. I mean, he don't look like a gunslinger."

They stepped down off the walk, and started across the street. They had taken but three steps when they heard the sharp rap of a shot. Clear, and ringing in the dark street. A shot, and then another.

"The Trail House!" Gates yelled, and broke into a run.

Kilkenny made the door two steps ahead of him, shoved it open, and stepped in. A cowpuncher lay on his face on the floor, a red stain growing on the back of his shirt. A drawn gun lay near his hand. He was dead.

Slowly Kilkenny looked up. Bert Polti stood across

the man's body, a smoking gun in his fist. He looked at Kilkenny and his eyes narrowed. Kilkenny could see the calculation in his eyes, could see the careful estimate of the situation. He had a gun out, and Kilkenny had not drawn. But there was Gates, and in his own mind, reading what the man thought, Kilkenny saw the momentary impulse die.

"Personal fight, Kilkenny," Polti said. "This wasn't no cattle war scrap. He knocked a drink out of my hand. I asked him to apologize. He told me to go to thunder and I beat him to it."

Kilkenny's eyes went past Polti to a cowpuncher from the Lord ranch.

"That right?" he demanded.

"Yeah," the cowpuncher said slowly, his expression unchanging, "that's about what happened."

Polti hesitated, then holstered his weapon and walked outside.

IX

Several men started to remove the body, and Kilkenny walked to the bar. Looking at the liquor in his glass, he heard Rusty speaking to him softly.

"The *hombre* that got hisself killed," Rusty said, "he was the one lookin' for you."

Kilkenny's eyes caught the eyes of the cowpuncher who had corroborated Polti and, with an almost imperceptible movement of the head, brought the man to the bar.

"You tell me," Kilkenny said. "What happened?"

The cowpuncher hesitated. "Ain't healthy to talk around here," he said doubtfully. "See what happened to one *hombre?* Well, he's only one."

"You don't look like you'd scare easy," Kilkenny said dryly. "You afraid of Polti?"

"No." The cowpuncher faced Kilkenny. "I ain't afraid of him, or of you, either, for that matter. Just ain't healthy to talk. Howsoever, while what Polti said was the truth, it looked powerful like to me that Polti deliberately bumped the cowboy's elbow, that he deliberately drew him into a fight."

"What was the 'puncher sayin'? Anythin' to rile Polti?"

"Not that I know of. He just said he had him a story to tell that would bust this country wide open. He did him a lot of talkin', I'd say."

So! Bert Polti had picked a quarrel with the man who had a message for Kilkenny, a man who said he could bust this country wide open. Kilkenny thought rapidly. What had the man known? And why from El Paso? Suddenly a thought occurred to him.

Finishing his drink, he said out of the corner of his mouth: "Stick around and keep your eyes open, Rusty. If you can, pick up Polti and stay close to him."

Stepping from the Trail House, Kilkenny walked slowly down the street, keeping to the shadows. Then he crossed the alley to the hardware store, and walked down its wall, then along the corral, and around it. He

180

moved carefully, keeping out of sight until he reached the hotel.

There was no one in sight on the porch, and the street was empty. Kilkenny stepped up on the porch and through the door. His action seemed leisurely, to attract no attention, but he wasted no time. The old man who served as clerk was dozing behind the desk, and the proprietor, old Sam Duval, was stretched out on a leather settee in the wide, empty lobby. Kilkenny turned the worn account book that served as register, and glanced down the list of names. It was a gamble, and only a gamble.

It was the fifth name down:

Jack B. Tyson, El Paso, Texas.

The room was number 22. Kilkenny went up the stairs swiftly and silently. There was no sound in the hall above. Those who wanted to sleep were already snoring, and those who wanted the bright lights and red liquor were already at the Trail House or the Spur.

Somewhere in his own past, Kilkenny now felt sure, lay the secret of the man in the cliff house, and this strange rider out of the past who had been killed a short time before might be a clue. Perhaps—it was only a slim chance—there was something in his war bag that would be a clue, something to tell the secret of his killing. For of one thing Kilkenny was certain—the killing of Tyson had been deliberate, and not the result of a barroom argument.

The hallway was dark, and he felt his way with his feet, then when safely away from the stair head, he struck a match. The room opposite him was number 14. In a few minutes he tried again, and this time he found room 22.

Carefully he dropped a hand to the knob and turned it softly. Like a ghost he entered the room, but even as he stepped in, he saw a dark figure rise from bending over something at the foot of the bed. There was a quick stab of flame, and something burned along his side. Then the figure wheeled and plunged through the open window to the shed roof outside. Kilkenny want to the window and snapped a quick shot at the man as he dropped from the roof edge. But even as he fired he knew he had missed.

For an instant he thought of giving chase, then the idea was gone. The man, whoever he was, would be in the crowds around the Spur or the Trail House within a matter of minutes, and it would be a fool's errand. In the meantime, he would lose what he sought here.

There was a pounding on the steps, and he turned, lighting the lamp. The door was slammed open, and the clerk stood there, his old chest heaving. Behind him, clutching a shotgun, was Duval.

"Here!" Duval bellowed. "What the consarn you doin' in there? And who's a-shootin'? I tell you I won't have it!"

"Take it easy, Dad," Kilkenny said, grinning. "I came up to have a look at Tyson's gear and caught somebody goin' through it. He shot at me."

"What right you got to go through his gear your ownself?" Duval snapped suspiciously.

"He was killed in the Trail House. Somebody told me he had a message for me. I was lookin' for it."

"Well, I reckon he ain't fit to do no kickin'," Duval admitted grudgingly, "and I heard him say he had a word for Kilkenny. All right, go ahead, but don't be shootin'! Can't sleep no-ways."

He turned and stumped down the narrow stairs behind the clerk.

A thorough examination of the drifting cowpuncher's gear got Kilkenny exactly nowhere. It was typical of a wandering cowpuncher of the period. There was nothing more, and nothing less.

There was still no solution, and out on the plains he knew there had been no settlement of the range war situation. His own warnings had averted a clash tonight, but he could not be everywhere, and sooner or later trouble would break open on the range. Already, in other sections, there was fighting over the introduction of wire. Here, the problem was made worse by the plot of the rustlers, or what he believed was their plot.

He could see a few things. For one, the plan had been engineered by a keen, intelligent, ruthless man. That he had already decided. It would have gone off easily had he not suddenly, because of Mort Davis, been injected into the picture. The fact that the mysterious man behind the scenes hated him was entirely

183

beside the point, even though that hate had evidently become a major motive in the mysterious man's plans.

Well, what did he have? Somewhere behind the scenes were the Brockmans. Neither of them was a schemer. Both were highly skilled killers, clansmen of the old school, neither better nor worse than any other Western gunmen except that they fought together. It was accepted by everyone that they would always fight together. The Brockmans he did not know. From the beginning he had accepted the fact that someday he would kill them. That he did not doubt. Few of the real gunfighters doubted. To doubt would have been to fail. There was the famous case of the duel between Dave Tutt and Bill Hickok as an example. Hickok shot Tutt and turned to get the drop on Tutt's friends before the man shot had even hit the ground. Bill had known he was dead.

The Brockmans no doubt felt as secure in the belief they would win as Kilkenny did. Somebody had to be wrong, but he could not make himself believe that was important. It was something he would have to live through, and it in no way could effect the solution of the plot on which he was working. True, he might be killed, but if so the solution wouldn't matter, anyway.

Every way he looked at it, the only actual member of the outlaw crew he could put a finger on was Bert Polti, and there was a measure of doubt there. He had not seen Polti at Apple Cañon. The man had a house there, but apparently spent most of his time at Botalla. Polti might have killed Wilkins and Carter. It seemed probable he had. Yet there was no proof. No positive proof.

Again and again Kilkenny returned to the realization that he must go up to the cliff house at Apple Cañon. He was not foolish enough to believe he could do it without danger. He had none of the confidence there that he would have in facing any man with a gun, for in the attack on the cliff house, an attack must be made alone. There were too many intangibles, too many imponderables, too many things one could not foresee. Lord and Steele might postpone their fighting for a day or two. They might never fight, but the problem of Lost Creek Valley would not be settled, and the man at Apple Cañon would try to force the issue at the first moment.

Standing in the dimly lit room, Kilkenny let his gaze drift about him. He had turned then, to go, when an idea hit him. The man who had fired at him before, and who had killed Carter, had stopped on the spot to reload. A careful man. But then, a smart man with a gun always was.

Carefully Kilkenny began to search the room, knowing even as he did that the search would be useless, for the man had left too quickly to have left anything. Then he went down the stairs and out back. With painstaking care, and risking a shot from the dark, he examined the ground. He found footsteps, and followed them.

Sixty feet beyond the hotel, he found what he sought. The running man had dropped the shell here, and shoved another into the chamber. Kilkenny picked up the brass shell. A glance told him what he had half expected to find. The unseen gunman was the man who had killed Sam Carter.

"Found somethin'?"

He straightened swiftly. It was Gates, standing there, his hand on his pistol butt, staring at him.

"A shell. Where's Polti?"

"Left town for Apple Cañon, ridin' easy, takin' his time."

"You been with him like I said?" Kilkenny demanded.

"Yeah." Rusty nodded. "He didn't do that shootin' a while ago if that's what you mean. I heard the shootin', then somebody come in and told us you was playin' target down here, and I'd had Polti within ten feet of me ever since you left me."

Kilkenny rubbed his jaw and stared gloomily into the darkness. So it wasn't Bert Polti. The theory that had been half formed in his mind that Polti was himself the unseen killer, and a close agent of the man on the cliff, was shattered.

Suddenly a new thought came to him. What of Rusty? Where had Rusty Gates been? Why had Rusty joined him? Was it from sheer love of battle and admiration for him, Kilkenny? Or for some deeper purpose?

He shook his head. He would be suspecting himself

if this continued. Turning, followed by Gates, he walked slowly back to the street. He felt baffled, futile. Wherever he turned, he was stopped. There were shootings and killings, then the killer vanished.

The night was wearing on, and Kilkenny mounted the buckskin and rode out into the desert. He had chosen a place, away from the town, for his camp. Now he rode to it and unsaddled Buck. Within a few minutes he had made his camp. He lit no fire, but the moon was coming up.

It was just clearing the tops of the ridges when he heard a ghost-like movement. Instantly he rolled over behind a boulder and slid his six-gun into his hand. On the edge of the wash, not fifteen feet away, a man was standing.

"Don't shoot, Kilkenny," a low voice drawled easily. "This is a friendly call."

"All right," Kilkenny said, rising to his full height. "Come on up, but watch it. I can see in the dark just as well as the light."

The man walked forward and stopped within four feet of Kilkenny. He was smiling a little.

"Sorry to run in on you thisaway," he said pleasantly, "but I wanted a word or two in private, and you're a right busy man these days."

Kilkenny waited. There was something vaguely familiar about the man. Somewhere, sometime he had seen him.

"Kilkenny," the man said, "I've heard a lot about you. Heard you're a square shooter, and a good man

187

to tie to. Well, I like men like that. I'm Lee Hall."

Lee Hall! The famous Texas Ranger, the man known as Red Hall who had brought law and order to more than one wild Texas cow town, and who was known throughout the border regions! He walked around a little, then stopped.

"Kilkenny," he said slowly, "I suppose you're wonderin' why I'm here? Well, as I said, I've heard a lot about you. I need some help, and I reckon you're the man. What's been happenin' down here?"

Briefly Kilkenny sketched in the happenings since his arrival, and what had happened before, from what he had heard. He advanced his theories about Apple Cañon.

"Nita Riordan?" Hall nodded. "I knew her old man. He came out from the East. Good man. Hadn't lived in Carolina long, came there from Virginia, but good family, and a good man. Heard he had a daughter."

"What did you want me t'do?" Kilkenny asked.

"Go ahead with what you're doin', and keep this cattle war down. I'm puttin' up wire on my own place now, and we're havin' troubles of our own. If you need any help, holler. But you're bein' deputized here and now. Funny thing," Hall suggested thoughtfully, "you tellin' me about the killin' of Wilkins and Carter. These ain't the first of the kind from the Live Oak country. For the past six years now people have been gettin' mysteriously shot down here. In fact, Chet Lord's half-brother was dry-gulched, and not far from Apple Cañon. Name of Destry King. Never found who did it, and there didn't seem any clue. But he told me a few days before he died that he thought he knew who the killer in the neighborhood was."

X

Hall left after over two hours of talk. Kilkenny stretched out with his saddle for a pillow, and stared up at the stars.

Could it be there was some other plot, something that had been begun before the present one? Could the old killings be connected with the new? There was only a hint. Destry King, half-brother to Chet Lord, had been killed when he had thought he had a clue. Had he confided in his half-brother?

It was high time, Kilkenny thought, that he had a talk with Chet Lord. So far circumstances had conspired to keep him so occupied that there had been no chance, and his few messages had been sent through Steve.

Long before daylight Kilkenny rolled out of his blankets and saddled up. He headed out for Cottonwood and the railroad and arrived at the small station to find no one about but the stationmaster. Carefully he wrote out three messages. One of them was to El Paso, and one to Dodge. The third was to a friend in San Antonio, a man who had lived long in the Live Oak country, and who before that had lived in Missouri.

When he left Cottonwood, he cut across country to

the Apple Cañon trail and headed for the Chet Lord Ranch. He was riding through a narrow defile among the rocks, when suddenly he saw two people riding ahead. They were Tana Steele and Victor Bonham.

"Howdy," he said, touching his Stetson. "Nice day."

Tana reined in and faced him.

"Hello," she said evenly. "Are you still as insulting as ever?"

"Do you mean, am I still as stubborn about spoiled girls as ever?" He grinned. "Bonham, this girl's shore enough a wildcat. Plenty of teeth, too, although pretty."

Bonham laughed, but Kilkenny saw his eyes drop to the tied-down guns. When they lifted, there was a strange expression in them. Then Bonham reined his horse around a bit, broadside to Kilkenny.

"Going far?" Bonham asked quietly.

"Not far."

"Chet Lord's, I suppose? I hear he's not a pleasant man to do business with."

Kilkenny shrugged. "Doesn't matter much. I do business with 'em, pleasant or otherwise."

"Aren't you the man who killed the Weber brothers?" Bonham asked. "I heard you did. I should think it would bother you."

"Bother me?" Kilkenny shrugged. "I never think of it much. The men I kill ask for it, an' they don't worry me much one way or the other."

"It wasn't a matter of conscience," Bonham replied dryly. "I was thinking of Royal Barnes. I hear he was

190

a relative of theirs, and one of the fastest men in the country."

"Barnes?" Kilkenny shrugged. "I never gave him a thought. The Webers asked for it, an' they got it. Why should Barnes ask for anything? I've never even seen the man."

"He might," Bonham said. "And he's fast."

Kilkenny ignored the Easterner and glanced at Tana. She had been sitting there watching him, a curious light in her eyes.

"Ma'am," he said slowly, "did you know Destry King?"

"King?" Tana's eyes brightened. "Oh, certainly. We all knew Des. He was Chet Lord's half-brother. Or rather, step-brother, for they had different parents. He was a grand fellow. I had quite a crush on him when I was fourteen."

"Killed, wasn't he?" Kilkenny asked.

"Yes. Someone shot him from behind some rocks. Oh, it was awful. Particularly as the killer walked up to his body and shot him twice more in the face and twice in the stomach."

Bonham sat listening, and his eyes were puzzled as he looked at Kilkenny. "I don't believe I understand," he said. "I thought you were averting a cattle war, but now you seem curious about an outdated killing."

Kilkenny shrugged. "He was killed from ambush. So were Sam Carter and Joe Wilkins. So were several others. Of course, they all cover quite a period of time, but none of the killin's was ever solved. It looks a bit odd."

Bonham's eyes were keen. He looked as if he had made a discovery. "Ah, I see," he said. "You imply there may be a connection? That the same man may have killed them all? That the present killings weren't part of the range war?"

"I think the present killin's was part of the range war," Kilkenny said positively, "but the way of killin' is like the killin's in them old crimes." He turned to Tana. "Tell me about Des King."

"I don't know why I shouldn't," she said. "As I told you, Des was a wonderful fellow. Everyone liked him. That was what made his killing so strange. He was a fast man with a gun, too, and one of the best riders on the range. Everyone made a lot of Des. Several riders had been shot, then an old miner. I think the first person killed was an old Indian. Old Comanche, harmless enough . . . used to live around the Lord Ranch. Altogether I think there were seven men killed before Des was. He started looking into it, having an idea they were all done by the same man. He told me once that I shouldn't go riding, that I should stay home and not ride in the hills. Said it wasn't safe."

"You rode a good deal as a youngster?"

"Oh, yes. There weren't many children around, and I used to ride over to talk and play with Steve Lord. Our fathers were good friends then, but it was six miles over rough country to his house then . . . wild country."

"Thanks. I'll be gettin' on. Thanks for the information, ma'am. Glad to have seen you again, Bonham."

Bonham smiled. "I think we may see each other often, Kilkenny."

Suddenly Tana put out her hand. "Really, Kilkenny," she said, "I'm sorry about that first day. I knew you were right that first time, but I was so mad I hated to admit it. I'm sorry."

"Shore." Kilkenny grinned. "But I'm not takin' back what I said about you."

Tana stiffened. "What do you mean?"

"Mean?" He raised his eyebrows innocently. "Didn't I say you were mighty pretty?"

He touched his spurs lightly to the buckskin's flanks and took off at a bound. After a brisk gallop for about a quarter of a mile he slowed down to a walk, busy with his thoughts.

Hall's information had been correct. Des King had had a theory as to who the killer was. He had been steadily tracking him down. Then the killer must have seen how near he was to capture, and had killed King. But what was the thread that connected the crimes? There was no hint of burglary or robbery in any of them. Yet there had to be a connection. The pattern was varied only in the case of King, for he had been shot several times, shot as if the killer had hated him, shot through and through. And why a harmless old Indian? A prospector? Several riders? Kilkenny rode on, puzzling.

Ahead of him the ground dipped into a wide and

shallow valley down which led the cattle trail he was following. Nearby were rocks, and a wash not far away.

Kilkenny rolled a smoke and thoughtfully lighted it. He flipped the match away and shoved his sombrero back on his head. The situation was getting complicated, and nowhere closer to a solution. The Steele and Lord fight was hanging fire. Twice there had been minor bursts of action, and then both had petered out after his taking a hand, yet it wasn't fooling anybody. The basic trouble was still there, and Davis hadn't been brought together with Steele and Lord.

Above the Live Oak, the country was seething, too. Wire cutters were loose, and fences were torn down nightly. Cattle were being rustled occasionally, but in small bunches. There was no evidence they had come through the Live Oak country and down to Apple Cañon.

Kilkenny had almost reached the Lord ranch house when he saw Steve come riding toward him, a smile on his face. Steve looked closely at Kilkenny, his eyes curious.

"Didn't expect to see you over here," he said. "I figgered you was goin' back to Apple Cañon!"

"Apple Cañon?" Kilkenny asked. "Why?"

"Oh, most people who see Nita want to see her again," Steve said. "You lookin' for Dad?"

"That's right. Is he around?"

"Uhn-huh. That's him on the roan hoss."

They rode up to the big man, and Kilkenny was pleased. Chet Lord was typically a cattleman of the old school. Old Chet turned and stared at Kilkenny as he approached, then looked quickly from him to Steve. He smiled and held out his hand.

"Kilkenny, huh? I thought so from the stories I been hearin'."

Lord's face was deeply lined, and there were creases of worry about his eyes. Either the impending cattle war was bothering Chet Lord or something else was. He looked like anything but a healthy man now. Yet it wasn't a physical distress. Something, Kilkenny felt instinctively, was troubling the rancher.

"Been meanin' to see you, Mister Lord," Kilkenny said. "Got to keep you an' Steele off each other's backs. Then get you with Mort Davis."

"You might get me and Webb together," Lord said positively, "but I ain't hankerin' for no parley with that cow-stealin' Davis."

"Shucks." Kilkenny grinned. "You mean to tell me you never rustled a cow? I'll bet you rustled aplenty in your time. Why, I have myself. I drove a few over the border couple of times when I needed a stake."

"Well, mebbe," said Lord. "But Davis come in and settled on the best piece of cow country around here. Right in the middle of my range."

"Yours or Steele's," Kilkenny said. "What the devil? Did you expect him to take the worst? He's an old buffalo hunter. He hunted through there while you was still back in Missouri."

"Mebbe. But we used this range first."

"How'd you happen to come in here? Didn't like Missouri?"

Chet Lord dropped a hand to the pommel of his saddle and stared at Kilkenny. "That's none of your cussed business, gunman! I come here because I liked it . . . no other reason."

His voice was sharp, irritated, and Kilkenny detected under it that the man was dangerously near the breaking point. But why? What was riding him? What was the trouble?

Kilkenny shrugged. "It don't mean anythin' t'me. I don't care why you came here. Or why you stay. By the way, what's your theory about the killin' of Des King?"

Chet Lord's face went deathly pale, and he clutched suddenly, getting a harder grip on the saddlehorn. Kilkenny saw his teeth set, and the man turned tortured, frightened eyes at Kilkenny.

"You better get," Lord managed after a minute. "You better get goin' now. If you'll take a tip from a friendly man, keep movin'."

He wheeled his horse and walked it away. For a moment, Kilkenny watched him, then turned his head to find Steve staring at him, in his eyes that strange, leaping white light Kilkenny had seen once before.

"Don't bother Dad," Steve said. "He ain't been well lately. Not sleepin' good. I think this range war has got him worried."

"Worried?"

"Uhn-huh. We need money. If we lose many cows, we can't pay off some debts we've got."

After a few minutes' talk, Kilkenny turned his buckskin and rode away from the ranch. He rode away in a brown study. Something about Des King had Chet Lord bothered. Was Lord the murderer of his own step-brother? But no! Chet might shoot a man, but he would do it in a fair, stand-up fight. There was no coyote in Chet Lord any more than there was in Webb Steele or Mort Davis.

XI

More and more the tangled skein of the situation became more twisted, and more and more he felt the building up of powerful forces around him, with nothing he could take hold of. He was in serious danger, he knew, yet danger was something he had always known. It was the atmosphere he had breathed since he had gunned his first man in a fair stand-up fight at the age of sixteen.

There was something about Chet Lord's fear that puzzled him. Lord had seemed more to be afraid for him, than for himself. Why? What could have aroused Lord's fear so? And what had made the man so upset? Was he really in debt? Somehow, remembering the place and the fat cattle, and knowing the range as he did, Kilkenny could not convince himself that Steve's statement was true. It was a cover-up for something else. There was fresh paint, all too rare in the Texas of those days, and new barbed wire, and new ranch buildings, and every indication that money was being spent.

Yet somewhere on that range a killer was loose, a strange, fiendish killer. It was unlike the West, a man who struck from ambush, a man who would kill an old Indian, who would ambush a prospector, and who would shoot down lonely riders. Somewhere, in all the welter of background, there was a clue.

Kilkenny lifted his head and stared gloomily down the trail. He was riding back through the shallow valley and down the cattle trail along which he had just traveled. He looked ahead, and for some reason felt uneasy.

Lord's gettin' his fear into me, he told himself grimly. *Still, in a country like this a man's a fool to ride twice over the same trail.*

On the impulse of the moment, he wheeled his horse and took it in two quick jumps for the shelter of the wash. As the horse gathered himself for the second jump, a shot sounded, and Kilkenny felt the whip of the bullet past his head. Then another and another.

But Buck knew what shooting was, and he hit the wash in one more jump and slid into it in a cascade o sand and gravel. Kilkenny touched spurs to the horse and went down the wash on a dead run. That wasl took a bend up above. If he could get around tha bend in a hurry, he might outflank the killer.

He went around the bend in a rush and hit th

ground running, rifle in hand. Flattening himself behind a hummock of sand and sagebrush, he peered through, trying to locate the unseen rifleman. But he moved slightly, trying to see better, and a shot clipped by him, almost burning his face. A second shot kicked sand into his eyes. He slid back into the wash in a hurry.

"The devil!" he exploded. "That *hombre* is wise! Spotted me, did he?"

He swung into saddle and circled farther, then tried again from the bank. Now he could see into the nest of rock where the killer must have waited and from which the first shot had come. There was no one in sight. Then he saw a flicker of movement among the rocks higher up. The killer was stalking him!

Crouching low, he waited, watching a gap in the rocks. Then he saw the shadow of a man, only a blob of darkness from where he huddled, and he fired. It was a quick, snapped shot and it clipped the boulder and ricocheted off into the daylight, whining wickedly.

Then it began—a steady circling. Two riflemen trained in the West, each maneuvering for a good shot, each wanting to kill. Twice Kilkenny almost got in shots, and then one clipped the rock over his head. An hour passed, and still he had seen nothing. He circled higher among the rocks and, after a long search, found a place where a man had knelt. On the ground nearby was a rifle shell, a shell from a Winchester carbine, Model 1873.

Mebbe that'll help, he told himself. *Ain't too many of 'em around. The Rangers mostly have 'em. And I've got one. I think Rusty still uses his old Sharps, and I expect Webb Steele does. But say!* He stopped, scowling. *Why, Tana Steele has a 'Seventy-Three! Yeah, and if I ain't mistaken, so has Bonham!*

This couldn't continue. Three times now the killer had tried shots at him, if indeed all had been fired by the same man. Bonham was in the vicinity, but why should Bonham shoot at him? Tana Steele was near, also, and Tana might have a streak of revenge in her system. But Chet Lord wasn't far away, either, and there were other men on the range who might shoot. Above all, this was an uncertain country where every man rode with an itch in his trigger finger these days.

One thing was sure. He was no nearer a solution than he had been. He had shells from the killer's six-gun and now from a Winchester 1873. Yet he had no proof beyond a hunch that the attempts at killing had been made by the same man.

The mysterious boss of Apple Cañon apparently had not wanted him killed. Hence, why the attempts now, if he were responsible? Or had the attempts, as he had suspected before, been the work of different men? But if not the Apple Cañon boss, and if not Bert Polti, then who? And why? Who else had cause to kill him?

Yet, so far as he knew, many of the mysterious killings in the past had been done without cause. At least, there had been no reason of which he was aware. Underneath it all, some strange influence was at work, something cruel and evil, something that was not typical of the range country where men settled their disputes face to face.

Kilkenny kept to back trails in making his way back to Botalla. The thing now was to get Steele, Lord, and Davis together and settle their difficulties if they could be settled. Knowing all three men, and knowing the kind of men they were, he had little doubt of a settlement.

The two bigger cattlemen were range hungry and Davis was stubborn. Like many men, each of them wanted to work his own way, each was a rugged individualist who had yet to learn that many more things are accomplished by co-operation than by solitary efforts.

Botalla lay quietly under the late sun when the buckskin walked down the street. A few men were sitting around, and among them were several cowpunchers from the Lord and Steele spreads. Kilkenny reined in alongside a couple of them. A short cowpuncher with batwing chaps and a battered gray sombrero looked up at him from his seat on the boardwalk, rolled his quid in his jaws, and spat.

"How's it?" he said carefully.

"So-so." Kilkenny shoved his hat back on his head and reached for the makings. "You're Shorty Lewis, ain't you?"

The short cowpuncher looked surprised. "Shore am. How'd you know me?"

"Saw you one time in Austin. Ridin' a white-legged roan hoss."

Lewis spat again. "Well, I'll be durned! I ain't had that hoss for three year. You shore got a memory."

Kilkenny grinned and lighted his cigarette. "Got to have, livin' like I do. An *hombre* might forget the wrong face!" He drew deeply on the smoke. "Shorty, you ride for Steele, don't you?"

"Been ridin' for him six year," Lewis said. "Before that I was up in the Nations."

"Know Des King?" Kilkenny asked casually.

Lewis got to his feet.

"Just what's on your mind, Kilkenny?" he asked. "Des King was a half-brother of Lord's, but we rode together up in the Nations. He was my friend."

Kilkenny nodded. "I thought mebbe. Lewis, I got me a hunch the *hombre* that killed Wilkins and Carter also killed Des King. I got a hunch that *hombre* tried to kill me."

"But King was killed some time ago," Lewis protested. "Before this fight got started."

"Right. But somebody is ridin' this range that has some other reason for killin' men. Somebody who's cold-blooded and vicious like nobody you ever seen Shorty. Somebody that's blood-thirstier than an Apache."

"What kind of man would be killin' like that?" Lewis demanded. Then he nodded. "Mebbe you got somethin', feller. Nobody would've shot into De after he was down, mebbe already dead, except some body who hated him poison mean, or somebody who loved killin'."

"There was an old Indian killed, and a prospector," reminded Kilkenny. "Know anything about them?"

"Yeah. Old Yellow Hoss was a Comanche. He got to hittin' the bottle purty hard and Chet Lord kept him around and kept him in likker because of some favor the old Injun done for him years ago. Well, one day they found him out on the range, shot in the back. No reason for it, so far's anybody could see. The prospector's stuff had been gone over, but nothin' much was missin' except an old bone-handled knife . . . a Injun scalpin' knife he used to carry. Had no enemies anybody could find. That seems to be the only tie up betwixt 'em."

"Where were they killed?"

"Funny thing, all of 'em were killed betwixt Apple Cañon and Lost Creek Valley. All but one, that is. Des King was killed on the Lord range not far from Lost Creek."

Kilkenny nodded. "How about you tellin' Chet to come in tomorrow mornin' for a peace talk, Shorty? 'll get Webb and Mort Davis in."

After he had told some of the Steele hands that he wanted to see Webb, Kilkenny rode down to the general store. Old Joe Frame was selling a bill of goods o Mort Davis's boy. Through him word was sent to Mort.

Rusty was waiting on the boardwalk in front of the rail House when Kilkenny returned. He looked up nd grinned.

"If you swing a loop over all three of 'em," he said, "you're doin' a job, pardner. It'll mean peace in the Live Oak."

"Yes," Kilkenny said dryly, "peace in the Live Oak after the gang at Apple Cañon is rounded up."

Gates nodded. Touching his tongue to a cigarette paper, he looked at Kilkenny. "May not be so hard. You been makin' friends, pardner. Lots of these local men been a-talkin' to me. Frame, Winston, the lawyer, Doc Clyde, Tom Hollins, and some more. They want peace, and they want some law in Botalla. What's more, they'll fight for it. They told me I could speak for 'em, say that when you need a posse, you can dang' soon get it in Botalla."

"Good." Kilkenny nodded with satisfaction. "We'll need it."

"Think any effort'll be made to break up your peace meetin'?" Rusty asked. "I been wonderin' about that."

"I doubt it. Might be. They better not, if they are goin' to try, because I got us a plan."

Morning sunlight bathed the dusty street when the riders from the Steele Ranch came in. There were just Webb, Tana, Weston, and two Steele riders. One o them was Shorty Lewis.

Rusty and Kilkenny were loafing in front of the Trail House.

"She's shore purty," Rusty said thoughtfully, staring after Tana as she rode toward the hotel. "Never saw a girl so purty."

Kilkenny grinned. "Why don't you marry the gal?" he asked. "Old Webb needs him a bright young son-in-law, and Tana's quite a gal. Some spoiled, but I reckon a good strong hand would make quite a woman of her."

"Marry *her?*" Rusty exploded. "She wouldn't look at me. Anyway, I thought mebbe you had your brand on her."

"Not me." Kilkenny shook his head. "Tana's all right, Rusty, but Kilkenny rides alone. No man like me has a right to marry and mebbe break some woman's heart when someday he don't reach fast enough. No, Rusty, I've been ridin' alone, and I'll keep it up. If I was to change, it wouldn't be Tana. I like to tease her a bit, because she's had it too easy with men and with everything, but that's all."

He got up, and together they walked down the street toward the hotel. Webb Steele and Tana were dling about the lobby. In a few minutes, Chet Lord came in, followed by Steve. Then the door opened, and Mort Davis stood there, his tall, lean figure almost blocking the door. He stared bleakly at Steele, hen at Lord, and walked across the room to stand efore the cold fireplace with his thumbs hooked in is belt.

"Guess we better call this here meetin' to order," Kilkenny suggested, idly riffling a stack of cards. "The way I hear it, Steele an' Lord are disputin' about ho fences in Lost Creek, while Mort here is holdin' ost Creek."

"He's holdin' it," Steele said harshly, "but he ain't got no right to it."

"Easy now," Davis said. "How'd you get that range of your'n, Steele? You just rode in an' took her. Well, that's what I done. Anyway, I figgered on Lost Creek for ten year. I come West with Jack Halloran's wagon train fifteen year ago and saw Lost Creek then."

"Huh?" Webb Steele stiffened. "You rode with Halloran? Why, Tana's mother was Jack Halloran's sister."

Davis stared. "Is that a fact? You all from Jackson County?"

"We shore are! Why, you old coot, why didn't you tell me you was *that* Davis? Jack used to tell us about how you and him. . . ." Webb stopped, looking embarrassed.

"Go right ahead, Steele," Kilkenny said dryly. "I knew if you and Mort ever got together and qui fightin' long enough to have a confab, you'd ge along. Same thing with Lord here. Now, listen. Ther ain't no reason why you three can't get together. You Steele, are importin' some fine breedin' stock. So i Lord. Mort hasn't got the money for that, but he doe have Lost Creek, and he's got a few head of stock. don't see why you need to do any fencin'. Fence ou the upper Texas stock, but keep the Live Oak countr this piece of it, as it is. Somebody has moved int Apple Cañon and has gathered a bunch of rustle around. Well, they've got to be cleared out. Loc stock, and barrel. I'm takin' that on myself."

"We need some law here," Webb Steele said suddenly. "How about you becomin' marshal?"

"Not me," Kilkenny said. "I'm a sort of deputy now. Lee Hall dropped by my camp the other night and he gave me this job. Makes it sort of official. But before I leave here, I'm goin' to take care of that bunch at Apple Cañon. Also," he added, "I'm goin' to get the man responsible for all these killin's."

His eyes touched Chet Lord's face as he spoke, and the big rancher's face was ashen.

Steve spoke up suddenly. "You sound as if you believed there's no connection between the killin's and this fight?"

"Mebbe there is, mebbe there isn't. What I think is that the man who's doin' the killin' is the same man who killed Des King, the same who killed old Yellow Horse."

XII

Chet Lord was slumped in his chair and Kilkenny thought he had never seen a man look so old. Tana Steele was looking strange, too, and Kilkenny, looking up suddenly, saw that her face was oddly white and puzzled.

"I think," Kilkenny said, after he had made his disturbing accusation about the mysterious killer, "that Des King knew who the killer was. He was killed to keep him from exposing that rattler, and also, I believe, because the killer hated King."

"Why didn't he tell then?" Steve Lord demanded.

Kilkenny looked up at Steve. "Mebbe he did," he said slowly. "Mebbe he did."

"What d' you mean by that?" Webb Steele demanded. "If he told, I never heard nothin' of it."

Kilkenny sat quietly, but he could see the tenseness in Tana's face, the ashen pallor of Chet Lord, slumped in his chair, and Steve's immobile, hard face.

"Des," Kilkenny said slowly, "had a little hang-out in the hills. In a box cañon west of Forgotten Pass. Well, Des kept a diary, an account of his search for the killer. He told Lee Hall that, and Lee told me. Tomorrow I'm goin' to that cabin in the cañon and get that diary. Then I'll know the whole story."

"I think . . . ," Tana began, but got no further because suddenly there was a hoarse yell from the street and the sharp bark of a six-gun. Then a roll of heavy firing.

Kilkenny left his chair with a bound and kicked the door open. There was another burst of firing as he lunged down the steps. His foot caught and he plunged headlong into the dust, his head striking a rock that lay at the foot of the steps.

Rusty and the others plunged after him. They were just in time to see two big men lunging for their horses while rifles and pistols began to bark from all over town. One of the big men threw up his pistol and blazed away at the group on the porch. Rusty had just time to grab Tana and push her against the wall as bullets spattered the hotel wall.

Kilkenny, his head throbbing from the blow of his fall, crawled blindly to his feet, eyes filled with dust. There was a wild rattle of hoof beats, then horses charged by him. One caught him a glancing blow with its shoulder and knocked him flat again. There was another rattle of gunfire, and then it was over.

Kilkenny got to his feet again, wiping the dust from his eyes.

"What was it?" he choked. "What happened?"

Frame had come running up the street from the general store carrying an old Sharps rifle.

"The Brockmans!" he shouted. "That's who it was! Come to bust up your meetin' and wipe you out, Kilkenny. Jim Weston, Shorty, and the other Steele rider tried to stop 'em."

Webb Steele stepped down, eyes blazing. "So that was the Brockmans that rode by! Cussed near killed my daughter!"

"Yeah," Frame agreed. "They got Weston. Lewis is shot bad, and they got the other boy . . . O'Connor, I think his name was. Weston never had a chance. He dropped his hand for his gun and Cain drilled him plumb center. Abel took Lewis, and they both lowered guns on the last one. It was short and bloody, and I don't think either of them got a scratch."

"This busts it!" Steele shouted. "We'll ride to Apple Cañon and burn that bunch to the ground! They've gone too far!"

Tana Steele was straightening up. She looked at Rusty. "You saved my life," she said quietly. "If you

209

hadn't thrown yourself in front of me, I might have been killed."

Rusty grinned, and suddenly Kilkenny saw blood on his shirt.

"You better take him inside, Tana," he said. "He' hit."

"Oh!" Tana caught Rusty quickly. "You're hurt!"

"It ain't nothin'," Rusty, said. "Shucks, I. . . ." He slumped limply against the wall.

Steele and Frame picked him up and started inside The Lords, father and son, headed down the street.

Suddenly Kilkenny heard the porch boards creak and a low voice, Bert Polti's, spoke.

"All right, Mister Lance Kilkenny, here's wher you cash in."

As Kilkenny recognized the voice, he whirled and drew. Polti's gun flamed as Kilkenny turned, and he felt the hot breath of the bullet. Then he fired.

Polti staggered, but caught himself. His head thrus forward, he tried to squeeze off another shot, but the six-gun wouldn't come up. He tried, then tried again but slowly the gun muzzle lowered, he toppled, and fell headlong.

Steele came charging to the door, gun in hand. H took one look, then holstered his gun.

"Polti, huh? He's had it a comin' for a long time How come he drew on you?"

Kilkenny explained briefly. Steele nodded. "Fig gered with your back turned he had a chance to ge you. Well, he didn't make it. Good work, son! Yo beat the rope for him with that bullet." He looked down at the fallen man. "Plumb center, too. Right through the heart."

Kilkenny looked up. "Steele, get your boys ready and stand by. Have Lord do the same. I'm goin' after the Brockmans myself, and, when I come back, we're goin' t'clean up Apple Cañon. Right now the main thing is to get the Brockmans out of the way."

"You goin' after 'em alone?" Steele was incredulous. "They just gunned down three men!"

"Uhn-huh." Kilkenny grinned, without humor. "But there's only two of 'em. I'll go after 'em. You see that somebody takes care of Rusty."

Steele grinned then. "I reckon Tana's doin' that."

A half hour later, stocked with grub for three days, Kilkenny rode out of town on the trail of the Brockmans. For the first half mile they had ridden hard, then had slowed down, saving their horses when they noticed no pursuit. They were both shrewd riders and they would save their horses while confusing their trail.

Three miles from town they had turned from the trail and taken to the rough country toward the lava beds. The trail became steadily more difficult, and wound back and forth across the desert, weaving around clusters of boulders and following dry washes. They had used every trick of desert men to lose their trail, and yet it could be followed. Still, time and again, Kilkenny was compelled to dismount from his horse, search the ground carefully, and follow as much by guess and instinct as by sight or knowledge.

It became evident the Brockmans were traveling in a big circle. Picturing the country in his mind, Kilkenny began to believe they were heading for Cottonwood. But why Cottonwood? Could they by chance know of the wires he had sent? Were they afraid of what those wires might mean to them? Or were they watching the station on orders from the unknown in the cliff house?

On impulse, Kilkenny swung the buckskin from the trail and cut across country for Cottonwood. Now he kept to the cover, and rode steadily by gulch and by cañon, toward the little station.

That night he bedded down on the same creek that ran into Cottonwood, but about six miles upstream from the town. His camp was a dark camp, and he tried no fire, eating a cold supper and falling asleep under the stars.

With daylight he was up. Carefully he cleaned his guns and reloaded them. He knew the Brockmans, and was under no misapprehension as to their skill. They were good, and they were dangerous together. If only by some fortune or stratagem he could catch each one alone. It was a thought, but the two ate together, slept beside each other, walked the streets together, and rode together.

It was almost nine o'clock before he saddled up and rode into town. If his calculations were correct, he was still ahead of the Brockmans. He would stil make Cottonwood first, but, if not first, at almost the same time.

When he reached town, he tied Buck under the trees on the edge of the stream, and walked across the little log footbridge to the street. There was nothing much in Cottonwood. On one side of the street was the little stream, never more than six feet wide, and a row of cottonwood trees backed by some bunches of willow beyond the stream. On the opposite side were the telegraph office and station, a bar, a small store, and four or five houses. That was about all. Kilkenny walked into the station.

"Any messages for me?" he asked.

The stationkeeper nodded and stretched. "Yeah. Just come in. Three of 'em."

He passed the messages across to Kilkenny, broke a straw off the broom, and began to chew it slowly and carefully, glancing out the window occasionally.

"Reckon there'll be some fireworks now," he said, nodding at the messages. "It shore beats the devil."

Kilkenny pocketed the messages without glancing at them, left the station, and crossed the street to the willows, after a brief glance into the bar. On the far side of the bridge he lay down on the grass and began to doze.

He was still there an hour later when the station-master came to the door. "Hossmen comin' out of the brakes, stranger!" he called out. "They look powerful like the Brockmans!"

Kilkenny got up slowly and stretched. Then he

leaned against the trunk of a huge cottonwood. Waiting.

The riders turned into the road leading to Cottonwood at a fast trot. There were three of them now. Kilkenny did not know the third man. They came on at a fast trot. As they reined in suddenly in front of the bar, Kilkenny stepped out and walked across the bridge.

Abel Brockman had swung down. Hearing the footsteps on the bridge, he turned and glanced over his shoulder. His hand stiffened, and he said something, low-voiced, and began to turn. The Brockmans had been caught off side.

Kilkenny stepped out quickly from under the trees. "All right!" he yelled.

Up the street a man sitting on a bench in front of a door suddenly fell backward off the bench and began to scramble madly for the door. Cain Brockman was still in the saddle, but he grabbed for his gun. As Abel's hand moved, Kilkenny's hand whipped down in the lightning draw that had made him famous. His gun came up, steadied, and even as Abel's six-shooter cleared his holster, Kilkenny fired.

Walking toward them he opened up with both guns. Abel got off a shot, but he had been knocked off balance by Kilkenny's first shot, and he staggered into the hitch rail. Cain's horse reared wildly, and the big man toppled backward to the ground. Kilkenny walked on, firing. Abel went to one knee, swung up, lurching, and his guns began to roar again.

Unbelieving, Kilkenny stopped and steadied his hand, then fired again. He was sure he had hit Abel Brockman with at least four shots.

Abel started to fall, and, swinging on his heel, Kilkenny tried to get a shot at the third man. But, grabbing Cain Brockman, the fellow dragged him around the corner out of sight. One of the horses trotted after them. Gun in hand, Kilkenny walked up to Abel.

Lying on his back in the dust, hand clutching an empty gun, his chest covered with blood, Abel Brockman stared at him.

"Cain'll kill you for this!" he snarled, his eyes burning. "Cain'll . . . oh!" Abel's face twisted with agony. "Cain . . . where's . . . ?"

One hand, thrust up and straining, fell into the dust, and Kilkenny, who had lifted his eyes toward the corner, started toward it.

Then he heard a sudden rattle of hoofs, and he broke into a run.

The third man, whoever he had been, with Cain Brockman across his saddle was taking off up the trail.

Kilkenny stared after them a moment, then shrugged, and walked back. He didn't think he had hit Cain Brockman. Probably he had been thrown from his horse and knocked cold.

Kilkenny retrieved Buck and swung into the saddle. Then he rode back by the station. The stationmaster thrust his head out.

"Didn't think you could do it, mister!" he said. "Some shootin'!"

"Thanks. And thanks for the warnin'." Kilkenny jerked his head back at Abel Brockman's body. "Better get that out of the street. He's pretty big and he'll probably spoil right fast."

He turned Buck toward the Botalla trail, and started down it. Well, it wouldn't be long now. He slapped Buck on the shoulder and lifted his voice in song:

I have a word to speak, boys, only one to say,
Don't never be no cow thief, don't never ride no stray.
Be careful of your rope, boys, and keep it on the tree,
But suit yourself about it, for it's nothin' at all to me!

Yet, even as he sang, he was thinking of the problems ahead. It was the time to strike now before anything else was done by the man at Apple Cañon to stir up strife between the Steele and Lord factions. If he and the ranchers and Botalla men could attack Apple Cañon and rout out the rustlers living in the long house there, and either capture them or send them over the border, much of the trouble would be over.

The cowpunchers of the two ranches would still have hard feelings, all too easily aroused if the proper stories were circulated and there should be more killing. Kilkenny realized that. So the thing to do was to strike before the man at the cañon could direct another move. That meant they must move at once—now!

XIII

Polti was dead. Abel Brockman was dead. That much at least had been done. Cain Brockman was alive. How would he react? Would he come out to kill Kilkenny as Abel had maintained? Would he flee the country, harassed by the thought of his brother's being gone? Would his confidence be ruined? There was no guessing what the man might do, and, despite the death of Abel, Kilkenny knew that Cain Brockman was still a dangerous man. Then two others remained, for Kilkenny was convinced that the unknown killer on the range and the man at Apple Cañon were not one and the same. Two men left, and no hint of who either one was.

On a sudden hunch, Kilkenny turned the buckskin and took a cut-off across the hills toward Apple Cañon. Another talk with Nita might give him some clue. Or was he fooling himself? Was it simply because he wanted to see the hazel-eyed girl who had stirred him so deeply?

He rode on, his face somber, thinking of her. A man who rode the lonely trails had no right to talk love to a woman. What did he have to offer? He had nothing, and always in the background was the knowledge that someday he would be too slow. He couldn't always win. Confident as he was, certain as he was of his kill, he knew that a day must come when he *would* be too slow. Either that, or it would be a shot in the back by an enemy, or a shot from someone who wanted to be able to say he was the man who killed Kilkenny. That was what any gunman of repute had always to fear. For there were many such.

More, there was that curious thing that made gunmen seek each other out to see who was fastest. Men had been known to ride for miles with only that in mind. Sometimes those meetings had come off quietly and without actual shooting. Sometimes it was a matter of mutual respect, as in the case of Wild Bill Hickok and John Wesley Hardin. Some gunmen did live together, some were friends, but they were the exception, and there was always the chance that some ill-considered remark might set off the explosion that might leave a dozen men lying in death.

No, men who lived by the gun died by the gun, and no such man had any right to marry. No matter where he might go in the West, there would always be someone, sometime, who would know him. Then his name would become known again, and he must either fight or be killed. Billy the Kid, Wild Bill, Ben Thompson, King Fisher, Phil Coe, and many another were to prove the old belief in dying by the gun. One day the time would come for him, too, and, until then, his only safety lay in moving on, in being what he had always been, a shadow on the border, a mysterious, little-known gunman who no man could surely describe.

The buckskin skirted the base of a hill, and came out among some cedars. Below lay Apple Cañon.

Thoughtfully Kilkenny studied the town. It seemed quiet, and there was no telltale flash from the cliff house. It might be that he could visit the town without being seen.

Carefully, keeping to cover of the scattered groves of cedar, Kilkenny worked his way along the mountainside, steadily getting closer and closer to the bottom. There was no sign of life.

Finally, close to the foot of the hill, he dismounted and tied the buckskin to a tree with a slipknot. Enough of a tie to let the buckskin know he should stand, but not enough to hold him if Kilkenny should whistle for him. Then, keeping the saloon between himself and the livery stable, Kilkenny walked casually out of the trees toward the back of the bar.

The biggest chance of being seen would be from the Sadler house, or by someone walking down the short street of the town. He made the trees around Nita's house without being seen. Carefully he placed a hand on the fence, then vaulted it, landing lightly behind the lilacs.

Inside the house someone was singing in a contralto voice, singing carelessly and without pretense as people sing when the song is from the heart more than the brain. It was an old song, a tender song, and for a long time Kilkenny stood there by the lilacs, listening. Then he moved around the bushes and stopped by the open window.

The girl stood there, just inside, almost within the reach of his arm. She had an open book in her hands, but she was not reading, she was looking out at the hills across the valley, out across the roof of the livery stable at the crags.

"It's a lovely picture," he said softly, "a mighty lovely picture. Makes me regret my misspent life."

She did not jump or show surprise, nor at first did her head turn. She kept her eyes on the distant crags, and smiled slowly.

"Strange that you should come now," she said softly. "I had been thinking of you. I was just wondering what you were like as a little boy, what your mother was like, and your father."

Kilkenny took off his hat and leaned on the window sill.

"Does it matter?" he asked softly. "No man is anything but what he is himself. I expect his blood has something to do with it, but not so much. It's what he does with himself, afterward. That's what matters. And I haven't done so well."

"No? I would say, Kilkenny, that you had done well. I would think you are an honorable man."

"I've killed men. Too many."

She shrugged. "Perhaps that is bad, but it is the West. I do not believe you ever shot a man from malice, or because there was cruelty in you. Nor do I believe you ever shot one for gain. If you killed, it was because you had to."

"That's the way I wanted it," he said somberly, "but it ain't always been that way. Sometimes you stand in a bar, and you see a man come in, and, when you look at him, you can tell by his eyes and his guns that he's a gunslinger. That's when you should leave. You should get out of there, but you don't, and then sooner or later you have to kill him. You have power when you can sling a gun, but it's an ugly power, and it keeps a man thinkin', worryin' for fear some day he may use it wrong."

"But Kilkenny," Nita said, "surely the West needs good men who can shoot. If there were only the bad men, only the killers, then what chance would honest people have? We need men like you. Oh, I know! Killing is bad, it's wrong. But here in the West men carry guns . . . for wild steers, for rattlesnakes, for Comanches or rustlers . . . and some learn to use them too well. But the West can't grow without them, Kilkenny."

He looked at her for a long moment. "You're a smart girl, Nita. You think, don't you?"

"Is that good, Kilkenny?" The hazel eyes were soft. "I'm not sure that a girl should ever think, or at least she shouldn't let a man know it."

"That's what they say." He grinned suddenly. "But not for me. I want a girl who can think. I want a girl to walk beside me, not behind me."

"Kilkenny," she said, and her hand suddenly came out to touch his, "be careful! He . . . he's deadly, Kilkenny. He's as vicious as a coiled snake, and he's living just for one thing now . . . to kill you! I don't think it is for the reason he gives. I think it is because he hates you for your reputation! I think he's a little afraid, too. He was drinking once, and he told me, when we were standing at the gate, that he wasn't afraid of Hardin. He said he knew he could beat Hardin or King Fisher. He said in all his life only two men had him bothered. Ben Thompson and you. He's always talking about you when he's drinking. He said Thompson had more nerve than any man he ever knew. And he said that, if you ever fought him, you'd have to be sure he was dead, because if he wasn't and he could walk, he'd come after you again. You bothered him because he said he couldn't place you. You were like a ghost. Nobody could say anything about you except that you were fast and hard-shooting."

Kilkenny nodded. "Yeah, I know what he means. When you're fast with a six-gun, you get to hearin' about others. After a while you get a picture of 'em in your mind, and, when you shoot, you shoot with that picture in mind. Most times you're right, too. But when you don't know about a man, it bothers you. A stranger rides in, wearin' his gun tied down, or mebbe two guns, and he's got a still, cold face, and he drinks with his left hand. Well, you know he's bad. You know he's a gun slick, but you don't know who he is It leaves you restless and uncertain. Once you know what he is, then you know what you're up against."

They stood there for a while in the warm sun, and a little breeze stirred, and the lilac petals sifted over hi shoulders, and he could smell their heavy perfume He looked up at the girl and felt a strange yearnin rise within him. It wasn't merely the yearning of man for a woman. It was the longing of a man for a home, for a fireside, for the laughter of children and the quiet of night with someone lying beside you. The yearning for someone to work for, to protect, someone to belong to, and some place in life where you fitted in.

It was so different from all he had known these last bitter years. These years of endless watchfulness, of continual awareness, of looking into each man's eyes, and wondering if he was another man you would have to kill, of riding down long trails, always aware that a bullet might cut you down. Yet, even as he thought of that, he knew there was something in his blood that answered to the wild call of the wilderness trails. There was something about riding into a strange town, swinging down from his horse, and walking into a bar, something that gave him a lift, and that gave life a strange zest.

There was something in the pounding of guns, the buck of a .45 in his hand, the leap of a horse beneath him, and the shouts of men, something that awakened everything that was in him. Times bred the men they needed, and the West needed such men, men who could bring peace to a strange, wild land, even while they found death for themselves. The West was won by gunmen no less than it was won by pioneering families, by fur traders and Indian fighters.

"What are you going to do, Kilkenny, when all this is over?" Nita asked softly.

He leaned his elbows on the window sill and

pushed his hat back on his head. "I don't rightly know," he said thoughtfully. "I reckon I'll just move on to some other town. Might rustle me a herd of cows and settle down somewheres on a piece of land. Mebbe over in the Big Bend country."

"Why don't you marry and have a home, Kilkenny?" Nita asked softly. "I think you'd make a good man around a home."

"Me?" He laughed, a bit harshly. "All I can do is sling a gun. That ain't much good around a house. Of course, I might punch cows, or play poker?" He straightened suddenly. "Time I was ridin' on. You be careful." Then he paused. "Tell me, Nita. What hold does this man have over you?"

"None. It is as I have said. I like to live, even here, and alone. I know I would die, and quickly, if I talked. Then, after a fashion, he has protected me. Of course, *señor*"—she fell into her old way of speaking—"it is that he wants me for himself. But I belong to no man. Yet."

"You can't tell me who he is?"

"No." She looked at him for a minute. "Perhaps you think I am not helping, but, you see, this is all I have this place. When it is gone, there is nothing. And the people out there"—she waved a hand toward Botalla—"do not think I am good. There would be no place for me there. I can only say that he will kill you if he can, and you must be careful if you go to the cliff. And do not go by the path."

When he was back on the buckskin, he turned

toward Botalla. If Steele and Lord had their men there, he would bring them back to Apple Cañon at once. In his ride to the place he had carefully scouted the approaches.

It had been easy enough to see just what they would be facing in an attack on the stronghold. He could muster about sixty men. There would be at least forty here at the cañon. Sixty wasn't really enough, for the men at the cañon would be fighting on their own ground, and behind defenses. And all were seasoned fighters. Nevertheless, much could be lost by waiting. The time was now. The raid on Apple Cañon, however, might leave the range killer at large.

As Kilkenny rode, his brain dug into the accumulated evidence, little as it was. Yet one idea refused to be denied, and it worried around in his mind until he reached town.

He came up to the Trail House at a spanking trot. Dropping from saddle, he flipped a dollar to a Mexican boy.

"Take that hoss, Pedro," he said, grinning, "and treat him right. Oats, hay, water, and a rub-down."

Pedro dropped his bare feet to the boardwalk and grinned, showing his white teeth.

"*Sí señor*, it shall be done!"

XIV

Rusty Gates was sitting inside the Trail House, holding himself stiffly, but grinning. Webb Steele was there, too. He looked up keenly as Kilkenny came in.

"Can't keep a good man down!" Rusty said. "Tana bandaged my side, and I wanted to give you a hand with the Brockmans, but she wouldn't let me. She's got a mind of her own, that girl!"

"What happened?" Frame demanded, stepping up.

"Got Abel," said Kilkenny. "Cain got thrown from his hoss. Knocked out, I think. Another *hombre* dragged him around a corner and got him aboard a hoss. They lit out, and I let 'em go."

Frame shook his head, his eyes dark with worry. "Cain will go crazy when he finds out Abel is dead and you're still alive. He'll come gunnin' for you, Kilkenny."

"He might." Kilkenny shrugged. "Got to take that chance. We're after bigger game now. We've got to wipe out that bunch at Apple Cañon. There's at least forty outlaws there."

"Probably more," Steele said. "Clyde Wilder was down there a few days ago, and he says there was anyways fifty, and might have been seventy."

"Don't make no difference," Frame declared "We're ready. Even Duval at the hotel is goin' Everybody wants to lend a hand."

Down the main street of Botalla there was suddenl

226

a pounding of hoofs, then a rider threw himself from saddle in front of the Trail House. He thrust the batwing doors open with his shoulder.

"Kilkenny!" he yelled. "Chet Lord's dyin'! Wants to see you, the worst way!"

"What happened?" Steele demanded.

"Gored by a crazy steer. Don't reckon he's got long. Askin' for Kilkenny. Don't know what he wants of him!"

"Steele," Kilkenny said, "get the men together, plenty of arms an' ammunition. Nobody leaves town to warn Apple Cañon. Get set to move, and, when you're ready, start her rollin'!"

He swung into saddle and turned the buckskin toward the Lord Ranch. His mind was working swiftly. What could Chet Lord have to say? That something had been worrying the big rancher for days was obvious enough, for the man had lost weight, he looked drawn and pale, and seemed to be under great strain.

Was he the unknown killer? As soon as that idea occurred, Kilkenny shook his head. The man was not the type. Bluff, outspoken, and direct, he was the kind of man who would shoot straight and die hard, but his shots would be at a man's face, not behind his back.

Kilkenny let the buckskin take his own gait. The long-legged horse knew his rider, and knew the mountains and desert. He knew that on many days he would be called on for long, hard rides, and had learned to pace himself accordingly. While cow ponies were held in light esteem, good as they might be, most cowpunchers had their favorites. Yet they were the gunmen and outlaws, the men whose lives might depend on the horses they rode, who really knew and cared for their horses. It was a time when a few such horses were to acquire almost as much fame as their hard-riding, straight-shooting masters. Sam Bass, for instance, was to become no more famous than the Denton mare he rode. And Black Nell, Wild Bill Hickok's horse with a trick of "dropping quick", was to save Hickok's life on more than one occasion. Kilkenny knew his buckskin, and Buck knew Kilkenny. During the years they had been together, they had learned each other's ways, and Buck had almost human intelligence when it came to knowing what his master wanted of him. He knew the ways of the frontier, and seemed to sense when there he could husband his strength, and when it must be used. Buck's ears were as perfect a guide to danger as a rifle shot. A flicker of movement, even miles ahead, and his ears were up and alert. And when he side-stepped, it was always with reason.

The Lord Ranch was strangely still when the buckskin cantered across the yard and came to a stop before the ranch house. Kilkenny swung to the ground and, leaving Buck ground-hitched, went up the steps at a bound.

Steve met him at the door. The young fellow's eyes were wet, and his face looked pale.

"He wants you," he said. "Wants you bad."

Kilkenny stepped through the door into the room where Chet Lord lay in bed. A sharp-eyed man with a beard stood up when Kilkenny walked in.

"I'm Doc Wentlow," he said softly, then smiled a little wryly. "From Apple Cañon. He wants to talk to you"—he glanced at Steve—"alone."

"Right."

The doctor and Steve went out, and Kilkenny watched them go. He saw Steve hesitate in the door as though loath to leave. Then the young cowboy stepped out, and Kilkenny turned to the old man lying on the bed. Lord's breathing was heavy, but his eyes were open. His face seemed to have aged, and he looked up at Kilkenny for a moment, then reached over and took his hand.

"Kilkenny," he whispered hoarsely, "I got a favor to ask. You got to promise me, for I'm a dyin' man. Promise me you'll do it. It's somethin' you can do."

"Shore," Kilkenny said gently. "If it's anything I can do, I will. You know that."

"Kilkenny," the old man's voice faltered, then his grip tightened on Kilkenny's wrist until the gun expert almost winced with the strength of it, "Kilkenny, I want you to kill my son."

"What?" Kilkenny stared. Then his eyes narrowed slowly. "Why, Lord?"

"Kilkenny, you got to. Kilkenny, I'm an old man, and, wrong or right, I love my boy. I love him like I loved his mother before him, but, Kilkenny, he's a

229

killer! He's insane! I've knowed it for months now! Des told me. Des King told me before Steve killed him. Long time ago, Steve had a bad fall off a buckin' hoss, and was unconscious for days and days. He was kind of queer when he got well, for a spell, then it looked like he was all right again, and didn't take pleasure in torturin' things no more. So when folks began to get killed around here, I never thought of the boy. Then I had a feelin', and one day Des come to me, and said he knowed Steve had done it, and that he'd have to be put away. He couldn't go on killin' folks. But then Des was killed, an' I couldn't bear to put Steve away. He . . . he . . . was all . . . I had, Kilkenny."

Kilkenny nodded slowly, looking down at the old man, seeing the pleading in his eyes, the plea for understanding, for sympathy at least.

"I done wrong. I knowed I was doin' wrong, but I hoped the boy would change. Sometimes he would be a good boy, then he'd get to moonin' around, then off he'd go."

For a long time the old man was silent, then his chest heaved and he turned his head.

"Kilkenny, you got to kill him. I won't be around no more to look after him, and you'll kill him decent Kilkenny. You'll shoot him, and he won't suffer. don't want him to suffer, Kilkenny. He's a baby fo pain. He can't suffer. I don't want him hung, neithe Kilkenny. Go shoot him down. I left a paper. It's in envelope, in case I die. Frame has got it. It tells a about it. Kilkenny, you got to kill him. I can't die thinkin' I've left that passel of evil behind me. An' but for that, he's been a good boy."

Kilkenny still stood staring down at old Chet Lord. Yes, it all fitted. Everything fitted. Steve had a Winchester 1873, and he could have done any of the shootings. Kilkenny had suspected something of the kind, which was why he had wired.

Wired?

Kilkenny clapped a hand to his pocket. Why, the wires! He'd had them in his pocket all the time! Hurriedly he dug into his pocket and pulled them out, unfolding the sheets.

The first was from San Antonio, and it was a verification of what Chet Lord had just told him, a few scattered facts about Steve's boyhood actions after his bucking horse accident, before his father had taken him away, all indicative of what might later come. That was unnecessary now. There would be evidence enough. His father's letter with Frame, and a few dates and times would piece it all together.

He unfolded the second message, from El Paso. As its message struck him, his hands stiffened.

TYSON SAW ROYAL BARNES AT APPLE CAÑON. HE KNEW BARNES FROM HAYS CITY AND ABILENE. BARNES MURDERED TYSON'S BROTHER, AND HE HEARD BARNES SWEAR TO KILL YOU FOR GETTING THE WEBERS. BE CAREFUL, KILKENNY, HE'S COLD AS A SNAKE, AND LIGHTNING FAST!

Kilkenny crumpled the message into a ball and thrust it into his pocket. The third message no longer mattered. It had only been an effort to learn what gun-slingers were where, in an effort to learn who was at Apple Cañon. Now he knew.

Royal Barnes! The name stood out boldly in his mind, and, even as he turned away from the old man on the bed, he saw that name, the name of a man he had never seen, the name of one of the most ruthless, cold-blooded killers in the West. A man as evil and vicious as any, yet reputed to be handsome, reputed to be smooth and polished, yet known to be a man filled with the lust to kill and of such deadly skill that it was said that Wes Hardin had backed down for him.

Kilkenny opened the door and stepped outside. Instantly Doc Wentlow got up.

"How is he?" he demanded.

"Pretty low." Kilkenny hesitated. "Where's Steve?"

"Steve? That was funny. He stood by the door a minute after you went in. Listening, I guess. Then all of a sudden he turned and got on a horse and took off, riding like the devil."

Despite himself, Kilkenny felt relieved. He had never killed a man unless the man was attempting to kill him. To walk out of the old cattleman's bed chamber and shoot Steve had been the furthest from his thoughts. Just what he had hoped to do, he was not sure. He did know that Steve Lord must be stopped.

Thinking back, he could remember the curiou

light, the blazing of some inner compulsion, which he had seen in Steve's eyes that first day in the Trail House. Yet Steve had not wanted to shoot it out with him, face to face. The young fellow was a man with an insane urge to kill. It grew from some inner feeling of inferiority. What Steve Lord would do now, Kilkenny could not guess. He knew killers, but the killers he knew were sane men, men whose thoughts could be read, and whose ways could be known. He did know that even the craziest man had his moments of sanity, and he knew that Steve Lord must have listened at the door, probably suspecting what his father intended to tell Kilkenny. So he had mounted and ridden away—to what? Where could he go? Yet even as the question came, he knew its answer. Steve Lord would go to Apple Cañon.

However insane the boy might be, there was some connection between him and the events stemming from the cañon rendezvous. And Kilkenny suspected that Steve had more than a little interest in Nita Riordan. But he would be riding now with fear in his heart, with desperation. For now he was in the open, the place he dreaded to be, where there was no concealment. He must fight, or he must die, and Kilkenny knew that such a man would fight like a cornered rat. Yet he had promised a dying man, and regardless of that it was something that had to be done.

Why should he feel depressed? Steve was a killer, preying upon the lonely and the helpless, a man who

233

shot from ambush, who killed from sheer love of killing. So he must be stopped. It was his own father, the man who sired him, who had passed sentence upon him.

Kilkenny turned off into the thick brush, unrolled his poncho, and was asleep almost as soon as he lay down.

XV

Botalla's Main Street was crowded with horsemen when Kilkenny rode back to the town. They were in for the finish, the lean, hard-bitten, wind- and gun-seasoned veterans of the Texas range. Riders from the Steele and Lord ranches, men who had ridden the long cattle trails north to Dodge and Abilene, men who knew the ways of cows and Indians and guns. Men who had cut their teeth on six-shooters.

Yet, as Kilkenny rode up the street, eyes alert for some sign of Steve Lord, he wondered how many o these men would be alive when another sundow came. For they were facing men as tough as them selves, as good, and as dangerous as cornered rats ar always dangerous. Vicious as men can be who fin themselves faced at last with justice and the necessit of paying for their misdeeds. They would figh shrewdly and well. They were not common criminal these men of Apple Cañon. A few, yes. But mar were just tough young men who had taken the wror trail or liked the hard, reckless life. A different turn events and they might have been satisfied cowhands, trail bosses, or they might have been Rangers. They would ask no quarter, and they would give none. They would fight this out to the last bitter ditch, and they would go down, guns blazing. They might have taken the wrong trails, but they had courage.

And for him? There was none of that; there was just one man. He had to mount that cliff and take Royal Barnes, the mysterious man in the cliff house. How would he know him? He did not know, but he did know that when he saw the man he would know him. Instinctively he knew that. When a man looked at another across a space of ground, with guns waiting, then he knew whether a man was fast and whether he would kill or not.

This would be different. Lance Kilkenny understood that. The Brockmans had been good but he had timed his chances to nullify their skill as a twin fighting combination. He had killed Abel Brockman as he had killed many another man, and most of them fast. But—and this he knew—he had never drawn against a man like Royal Barnes. Blinding speed. Barnes had that. Barnes had killed Blackie Slade, and Kilkenny recalled Slade only too well. He had seen Slade in action, and the man had been poison. Yet Barnes had shot him down as if he were an amateur.

Yet Kilkenny could feel something building up inside himself, and recognized what it was. It was his own compulsion, his own fire to kill. Every gunman had it. Without it, he was helpless. It was a fiery drive, but with it the cold ruthlessness of a man who knew he must kill, or he must die himself.

He swung down from his horse and walked into the Trail House.

"We're all set," Webb Steele said, walking forward. "All set, and ra'rin' to go. The boys wanted to wait and see how Chet is."

Kilkenny looked up. "Steele," he said slowly, "Chet's dyin'. He told me about the killin's. It's Steve. Steve's a killer!"

Webb Steele stared, and Frame rubbed the back of his hand across his eyes.

"Huh!" Steele said. "I might of knowed it! He was always a strange 'un."

"That ain't all," Kilkenny said quietly. "The man up in the cliff house is Royal Barnes."

"Barnes?" Rusty Gates's face tightened, then turned gray as he looked at Kilkenny. "One of the slickes *hombres* that ever threw a six-gun."

In the stillness that followed men stared at one another and into the mind of each came stories they had heard of Royal Barnes and of the men who had gone down before his roaring guns. In the mind of each was a fear that he might be next.

The silence was shattered by the crashing of a door and as one man the crowd turned to stare at the rear door of the Trail House. Several steps inside the door, his head thrust forward and his eyes glaring with killing hatred, stood a huge, broad-jawed man a checked shirt and black jeans stuffed into heavy cowhide boots.

"Cain Brockman!" Frame yelled.

The big man strode forward until he stood only three paces from Kilkenny. Then, with cold, merciless hatred in his eyes, he unbuckled his belt and shed his guns.

"I'm goin' to kill you, Kilkenny! With my bare hands!"

"No!' Webb burst out, thrusting himself forward. "We got us a job to do, Kilkenny!"

"Keep out of this," Kilkenny said quietly.

Without further word and without taking his eyes from Cain's, he unbuckled his own belt and passed his guns to the big rancher.

With a hoarse grunt, Cain Brockman lunged, swinging a ponderous right fist. Kilkenny stepped inside and snapped a lightning left to the face, then closed with the big man, slamming both fists to his midriff. Cain grabbed Kilkenny and hurled him across the room so that he brought up with a crash against the bar. Cain lunged after him.

Kilkenny pivoted away, stabbing a left that caught the bigger man on the cheek bone, then Brockman swung and caught Kilkenny with a hard right swing that knocked him to his knees. A kick aimed at Kilkenny's shoulder just grazed him as he was starting to rise. He lost balance, toppling over on the floor. He rolled away and came up swinging, and the two sprang together.

Brockman's face was savage with killing fury and an ugly glee at having his enemy and the man who had slain his brother actually in his hands. Another right caught Kilkenny a glancing blow, but he weathered it and stepped under a left, slamming a right to the ribs. Then he hooked a left to the chin, leaping away before Cain could grab him.

It was toe-to-toe, slam-bang fighting, and neither man was taking any precaution. Both fought like savages, and Kilkenny's face became set in a mask of fierce desperation as he met charge after charge of the huge Brockman. They stood, straddle-legged, in the middle of the floor and swung until the smacking sound of their blows sounded loudly in the room and blood streamed from cut and battered faces. Brockman was a brute for strength, and he was out for a kill, filled with so much fury that he was almost immune to pain.

Kilkenny stepped inside a right and ripped his own right to the heart. He hooked both hands to the body then they grappled and went to the floor, kicking and gouging. There were no rules here, no niceties of combat. This was fighting to maim, to kill, and there was only one possible end—the finish of one or the other.

Blood streaming from a cut on his cheek, Kilkenny lanced a left to the mouth, then missed a right and took a wicked left to the middle. But he took the punch going in, punching with both hands to the head.

Cain's big head rocked with the force of the blows and he spat a tooth onto the floor, and swung hard to the head, staggering Kilkenny. The gunman came back fast, ripping a right uppercut to the chin, then a left and right to the head. Kilkenny was boxing now. Long ago he had taken lessons from one of the best fighters of the day, and he found now that he needed every bit of his skill.

It was not merely a matter of defeating Cain Brockman. After that, and perhaps soon, he would be meeting Royal Barnes, and his hands must be strong and ready. He stepped inside of a right and smashed a right to the bigger man's body, then hooked a left to the heart, and drummed with both hands against the big man's torso. Body punches stood less chance of hurting his hands, and he must be careful.

He stepped around, putting Brockman off side, and then crossed a right to Cain's bleeding eye, circled farther left, and crossed the right again. Then he stabbed three lefts to the face, and, as Cain lunged, he stepped inside and butted him under the chin with his head.

Brockman let out a muffled roar and crowded Kilkenny to the bar, but Lance wormed away and slugged the big man in the ribs. Brockman was slowing down now, and his face was bloody and swollen. His eyes gleamed fiercely, and he began to move slowly, more cautiously, moving in, watching for his chance.

Cain backed up, backed slowly, trying to keep away

from that stabbing left, then suddenly he brought up against the wall. Putting a foot against the wall, he shoved himself off it like a huge battering ram and caught Kilkenny fully in the chest with his big head. Kilkenny went crashing to the floor!

Brockman rushed close, trying to kick him in the ribs, but Kilkenny got to his hands and knees and hurled himself against Brockman's legs. The big man tumbled over him, then spun on the floor with amazing agility and grabbed Kilkenny's head, groping for his eyeballs with his thumbs!

Mad with pain and fear for his eyes, Kilkenny tore loose and lunged to his feet. Brockman came up with him and Kilkenny stabbed a powerful left into that wide granite-hard face. Blood flew in every direction, and he felt the nose bone crunch under his fist. With a cry of pain, Cain Brockman lunged forward, and his mighty blows pounded at Kilkenny's body. But the lighter man blocked swiftly and caught most of the blows on his elbows and shoulders. Driven back, the gun expert swayed like a tree in a gale, fighting desperately to set himself, to stave off that terrific assault. There was the taste of blood in his mouth and he felt his lungs gasping for breath, and their gasping was a tearing pain.

Brockman closed in and thrust out a left that might have ended the fight, but Kilkenny went under it and butted Cain in the chest, staggering the bigger man. Missing a right hook to the head, Kilkenny split Brockman's cheek wide open with his elbow, ripped the elbow back, slamming the big man's head around.

Despite the fierceness of the fighting, Kilkenny was not badly hurt. Most of the bigger man's blows had been wasted. One eye was cut, and he knew his jaw was swollen, but mainly he was fighting to stave off the big man's fierce attacks. They swept forward with tremendous power, but little skill. Yet Kilkenny was growing desperate. His punches seemed to have no effect on the huge hulk of Cain Brockman. The big man's face was bleeding from several cuts. His lips were battered, and one eye was badly swollen, but he seemed to have got his second wind, and was no less strong than when he had thrown his first punch. On his part, Kilkenny had one eye almost swollen shut. He could taste blood from a cut inside his mouth, and his breath was coming in those tearing gasps.

Brockman bored in, swinging. Kilkenny pushed the left swing outward and stepped in, bringing up a hard left uppercut to the wind that stopped Brockman in his tracks. But the big man bowed his head and lunged. Kilkenny dropped an open palm to the head and shoved the fellow off balance, and, as his guard came down for an instant, he stabbed a left to Brockman's cut eye. Then he circled warily.

Cain lunged, kicked at Kilkenny's middle. The lighter man jerked back, then stepped off to the left, and dived in a long flying tackle. He hit Brockman at the knees, grabbed, and jerked hard! Brockman came down with a *thud*, his head bouncing on the wood floor. Kilkenny rolled free and scrambled to his feet. Brockman was getting up, but he was slow. Half up, he lunged in a long dive himself, but Kilkenny jerked his knee into the big man's face. Cain rolled off to one side, his face bloody and scarcely human. Yet even then he tried to get up.

He made it. Kilkenny was sick of the fight, sick of the beating he was giving the bigger man. He stepped in, measured him with a left, and, when Cain tried to lift his hands, Kilkenny slugged him in the solar plexus. The big man went down, conscious, but paralyzed from the waist down.

Kilkenny stepped back, weaving with exhaustion. Grimly he worked his battered, stiffened hands.

"You ain't in shape for that raid now, Kilkenny," Rusty expostulated. "Better call it off or stay behind."

"To thunder with that," Kilkenny replied sharply. "I want Royal Barnes myself, and I'll get him."

Walking back to the wash basin, he dipped up water from the bucket and bathed his cut and bruised face. He turned his head as Frame walked up, his face grave.

"Get me some salts," Kilkenny said.

While he waited, he bathed his hands and replaced his torn shirt with one brought him by Gates.

When he had the salts, he put them in hot water one of the men brought and soaked them. He knew there was nothing better for taking away soreness and stiffness, and it was only his hands he was worried about. He was bruised and battered, but not seriously

Although that one eye was swollen, he could still see through the slit.

Finally he straightened. He turned and looked at the men around him. They would never ride without him, he knew, or, if they did, their hearts wouldn't be in it. He laughed suddenly.

"All-l-l set!" he yelled. "Let's ride!"

XVI

On Buck, Kilkenny headed toward the Apple Cañon trail. He was tired, his muscles were weary and heavy, yet he knew that the outdoor life he had lived, and the rugged existence he had known most of his life would give him the stamina he needed now. Behind him a tight cavalcade of grim, mounted men were riding out to battle.

Rusty Gates rode up alongside Kilkenny in the van of the column.

"You had yourself a scrap," Rusty said. "Can you see?"

"Enough."

"How about your hands?" Gates noticed the swollen knuckles and his lips tightened. "Kilkenny, you can't drag a fast gun with hands like that. Facin' Barnes will be suicide."

"Nevertheless, I'm facin' him," Kilkenny said crisply. "He's my meat, and I'll take him. Besides, my hands ain't as bad as they look, and most of that swelling will be gone soon. It ain't goin' to be speed that'll win, anyway. Both of us are goin' to catch lead. It'll be who can take the most of it and keep goin'." He nodded. "The way I figure it we'll be spotted before we get there. They'll be holed up around the buildin's. The bunkhouse, the livery stable, and blacksmith shop all looked like they was built to stand a siege."

"They were," said Rusty. "Heavy logs or stone, and built solid. Bill Sadler's place, on the same side as the Border Bar, is 'dobe, and it has walls three feet thick. Them windows was built to cover the trail, an' believe me, it ain't a goin' to be no picnic gettin' tough men out of there."

"I know." Kilkenny rubbed Buck's neck thoughtfully. "Got to figger that one out. I'm thinkin' of leavin' you fellers anyway. I'm goin' up to the castle."

"Alone?" Gates was incredulous. "Man, you're askin' for it. He'll be forted up there, and plenty tight."

"I doubt it. I doubt if he ever lets more than one man up there with him. Royal Barnes, as I hear of him, ain't a trustin' soul. No, I'm goin' to try comin down the cliffs above the castle."

"The what?" Gates swore and spat into the road "Holy snakes, feller! They're sheer rock! You'd need a rope and a lot of luck. Then he'd see you and ge you before you ever got down!"

"Mebbe, I got the rope, and mebbe the luck Anyway, I'm comin' down from behind where h won't be expectin' me, an' I'm comin' down while you fellers are hard at it in front. Now here . . . the way I see it. . . ."

As Webb Steele, Frame, and Rusty listened, he outlined a brief plan of attack. At the end, they began to grin.

"Might work," observed Steele. "I'd forgot that claim up in the pass. If that stuff is still there. . . ."

"It is. I looked."

Kilkenny had no illusions about the task ahead. With the plan he had conceived, carefully working it out during the previous days, he believed that the fort houses of Apple Cañon could be taken. It meant a struggle, and there would be loss of life. This riding column would lose some faces, and there would be hectic and bloody fighting before that return.

Where was Steve Lord? Had Steve risen to his bait and ridden to the hidden cabin in the box cañon? It would be a place to find him, and there, if Steve should go for a gun, he could end it all. Kilkenny shrank from the task, and only the knowledge that other people would die, brutally murdered from ambush, made him willing to go through with keeping his promise to old Chet Lord. He had that job to do, and luckily the cañon was only a short distance from the route the cavalcade would follow.

There had been no diary left by Des King. The idea had been created in Kilkenny's own mind. It had been bait dropped for the killer, and it had been conceived even before Kilkenny had known that Steve was the man. That he would have discovered it soon, he knew, for slowly the evidence had been mounting, and he had been suspicious of Steve Lord, waiting only for a chance to inspect his guns and check them against the shells he had picked up as evidence.

What would Steve Lord do now? To all intents, he would be outlawed. He knew his father had exposed him, and he must realize there was evidence enough to convict him, or to send him to an asylum. He would be desperate. Would he try to kill Kilkenny? To escape? Or would he go on a killing spree and gun down everything and everybody in sight? Kilkenny couldn't escape the feeling that Steve would go to Apple Cañon. He turned suddenly to Webb Steele.

"I'm ridin' for the shack where I let Steve think Des King hid his diary," he said. "If I ain't back when you get to Apple Cañon, just go to work and don't wait for me. I'm goin' to get Steve Lord. When I find him, I'll come back."

He wheeled the buckskin and took off up a draw into the deeper hills. He had been thinking of this route all the way along. He wasn't sure this route would do it, but knew he could find a way.

The draw opened into a narrower draw, and after a long time he rode out of that to a little stretch o bunch grass that led away to a ridge covered wit cedar and pine. It was cool among the trees, and h stopped for a minute to wipe his hatband and chec his guns once more. Then he slid his Winchester fror the scabbard and took it across the saddle in front c him. His hands felt better than he had expected they would.

He struck a path and followed it through the trees, winding steadily upward. Then the trees thinned, and he entered a region of heaped-up boulders among which the trail wound with all the casualness of cow trails in a country where cows are in no hurry. Twice rabbits jumped up and ran away from his trail, but the buckskin's hoofs made no noise on the pine needles or in the dust of the boulder-bordered trail.

Kilkenny was cutting across a meadow when he saw the prints of a horse bisecting the trail he was making. In the tall grass of the meadow he could tell nothing of the horse, but on a hunch he turned the buckskin and followed. Whoever the rider was, he was in a hurry, and was moving in as straight a line as possible for his objective.

It had bad features, this trailing of a man native to the country. Such a man would know of routes, of places of concealment of which Kilkenny could know nothing. Such an advantage could mean the difference between life and death in such a country.

Scanning every open space before he moved across t, Kilkenny followed warily. He knew only too well he small amount of concealment it required to prevent a man from being seen. A few inches of grass, lothes that blended with surroundings, and immoility was all that was essential to remain unseen.

Sunlight caught the highest pinnacles of the mountains beyond Forgotten Pass, and slowly the long shadows crept up, and the day crept away down the cañons. Kilkenny rode steadily, every sense alert for trouble, his keen eyes searching the rocks ahead, roving ceaselessly, warily.

The cabin was not far away when he dismounted and faded into the darkness under the gnarled cedars, and looked down through the narrow entrance between the cliffs into the box cañon.

A squat, shapeless structure, built hurriedly by some wandering prospector or hopeful rancher in some distant period. Then in the years that followed it had slowly sagged here and there, the straw roof rotting and being patched with cedar bows, earth, and even heavy branches from the cedars until the roof had become a mound. It was an ancient, decrepit structure, its one window a black hole, its door too low for a tall man. About it the grass was green, for there was a stream nearby that flowed out of the rocks on one side and returned into the cliffs on the other, after diagonally crossing the cañon and watering a meadow in transit.

Outside the shack, under an apple tree, stood a saddled horse, his head hanging.

Well, here we are, Kilkenny, he told himself dryly *Now to get close.*

Leaving the buckskin in concealment, Kilkenny went at a crouching run to the nearest boulder. Ther he ran closer, crouched behind some cedars, watchin; the cabin.

He was puzzled. There was still no movement.

should take no time to find there was nothing in the cabin, and it was black in there. He should have seen a light by now, for there was no use trying to search in the blackness inside that cabin for anything.

The saddled horse stood, his head low, waiting wearily. A breeze stirred leaves on the cottonwood tree, and they whispered gently. Kilkenny pulled his sombrero lower and, moving carefully with the whispering of the leaves to cover the rustle of his movement, worked along the cliff into the bottleneck entrance. Slowly, carefully he worked inside.

There was no shot, no sound. In dead silence he moved closer, his rifle ready, his eyes searching every particle of cover. The horse moved a little, and began cropping grass absently, as though it had already eaten its fill.

Suddenly he had a feeling that the cabin was empty. There was no reason for him to wait. He would go over to it. He stepped out, his rifle ready, and walked swiftly and silently across the grass toward the cabin.

The horse stopped cropping grass and looked up, pricking its ears at him. Then he stepped up to the cabin.

Was there anyone inside? The blackness of the squat cabin gave off no sound. Despite himself, Kilkenny felt uneasy. It was too still, and there was something unearthly about this lost cañon and the lonely little shack. Carefully he put down his rifle and slipped a six-gun into his hand. The rifle would be a handicap if he had to fight in the close quarters of the shack. Then he looked in.

It was black inside, yet between himself and the hole that passed for a window he could see the vague outline of a sleeping man's head. A man's head bowed forward on his chest.

"All right," he said clearly. "You can get up and come out!"

There was neither sound nor movement. Kilkenny stepped inside quickly, and there was still no move. Taking a chance, he struck a match. The man was dead.

Searching about, he found a stump of candle that some passing rider had left. Lighting it, he looked at the man. He was a stranger. A middle-aged man, and a cowhand by his looks. He had been shot in the right temple by someone who had fired from outside the window. The room had been thoroughly ransacked.

Kilkenny scowled. An innocent man killed, and his fault. If he hadn't told that story, this might not have happened. But at the time he had needed some way for the killer to betray himself. It wasn't easy to do everything right.

He walked out quickly and swung into saddle There was nothing to do now but to return. He coul make it in time, and morning would be the time t attack. In the small hours, just before daylight.

Buck took the trail with a quickened step as thoug he understood an end was in sight. Kilkenny lounge in the saddle. Steve would be riding hard now. He would be heading for Apple Cañon.

Weary from the long riding and the fight with Cain Brockman, Kilkenny lounged in the saddle, more asleep than awake. The yellow horse ambled down the trail through the mountains like a ghost horse on a mysterious mission.

There was a faint light in the sky, the barest hint of approaching dawn, when Kilkenny rode up to join the posse. They had stopped in a shallow valley about two miles from Apple Cañon. Dismounted, aside from guards, they were gathered about the fire.

He swung down from his horse and walked over, his boots sinking into the sand of the wash. The fire-light glowed on their hard, unshaven faces.

Webb Steele, his huge body looking big as a grizzly's, looked up.

"Find Steve?" he demanded.

"No. But he killed another man." Briefly Kilkenny told of what he had found at the cabin. "Steve's obviously come on here. He's somewhere in there."

"You think he worked with this gang?" Frame asked. "Against his own pa?"

"Uhn-huh. I think he knows Barnes. I think they cooked up some kind of a deal. I think Steve Lord has a heavy leanin' toward Nita Riordan, too. That's mebbe why he come here."

Rusty said nothing. He was looking pale, and Kilkenny could see that the ride had been hard on him. He shouldn't have come with that wound,

Kilkenny thought. But men like Rusty Gates couldn't stay out of a good fight. And wounded or not, he was worth any two ordinary men.

Not two like Webb Steele, though. Or Frame. Either of them would do to ride the river with. They might be bull-headed, they might argue and talk a lot, but they were men who believed in doing the right thing, and men who would fight in order to be able to do it.

XVII

Glancing around at the others, Kilkenny saw that they looked efficient and sure. All of those men had been through the mill. There probably wasn't a man in the lot who hadn't fought Comanches and rustlers. This was going to be tough, because they were fighting clever men who would kill, and who were fighting from concealment. It is one thing to fight skilled fighting men, who know Indian tactics, and to fight those who battle in the open.

"Well," Kilkenny said, as he tasted the hot, bitter black coffee, "we got to be movin'. The stars are fadin' out a little."

Webb Steele turned to the men.

"You all know what this is about," he said harshly "We ain't plannin' on no prisoners. Every man who wants to surrender will get his chance. If a man throws down his shootin' iron, take him. We'll try 'em decent, and hang the guilty ones. Although," h added, "ain't likely to be any innocent ones in Apple Cañon."

"One thing," Kilkenny said suddenly. "Leave Nita Riordan's Border Bar and her house alone."

He wasn't sure how they would take that, and he stood there, looking around. He saw tacit approval in Rusty's eyes, and Steele and Frame nodded agreement. Then his eyes encountered those of a tall, lean man with a cadaverous face and piercing gray eyes. The man chewed for a minute in silence, staring at Kilkenny.

"I reckon," he said then harshly, "that if we clear the bad 'uns out of Apple, we better clear 'em all out. Me, I ain't stoppin' for no woman. Nor that half-breed man of her'n, neither!"

Steele's hand tightened, and his eyes narrowed. Kilkenny noticed tension among the crowd. Would there be a split here? He smiled. "No reason for any trouble," he said quietly, "but Nita Riordan gave me a tip once that helped. I think she's friendly to us, an' I think she's innocent of wrong doin'."

The man with the gray eyes looked back at him. "I aim to clear her out of there as well's the others. I aim to burn that bar over her head."

There was cruelty in the man's face, and a harshness that seemed to spring from some inner source of malice and hatred. He wore a gun tied down, and had a carbine in the hollow of his arm. Several other men had moved up behind him now, and there was a curious similarity in their faces.

253

"Time to settle that," Kilkenny said, "when we get there. But I'm thinkin', friend, you better change your mind. If you don't, you're goin' to have to kill me along with her."

"She's a scarlet woman," the man said viciously, "and dyin's too good for her kind. I'm a gettin' her, and you stay away."

"Time's a-wastin'," Steele said suddenly. "Let's ride!"

In the saddle, Kilkenny swung alongside of Steele in the van of the column.

"Who is that *hombre?*" he demanded.

"Name of Calkins. Lem Calkins. He hails from West Virginia . . . lives up yonder in the mountains. He's a feuder. You see them around him? He's got three brothers, and five sons. If you touch one of 'em, you got to fight 'em all."

They rode up the rise before coming to Apple Cañon, and then Kilkenny wheeled his horse toward the cliff. Almost instantly a shot rang out, and he wheeled the buckskin again and went racing toward the street of the town.

More shots rang out, and a man at the well dropped the bucket and grabbed for his gun. Kilkenny snapped a shot and the man staggered back, grabbing at his arm. A shot ripped past Kilkenny, scarring the pommel of his saddle as he lunged forward. He snapped another shot, then raced the buckskin between Nita's house and the Border Bar, dropping from the saddle.

He was up the back steps in two jumps, and had swung open the door. Firing had broken out in front, but Kilkenny's sudden attack from the rear of the bar astonished the defenders so much that he was inside the door before they realized what was happening. He snapped a shot at a lean, red-faced gunman in the door. The fellow went down, grabbing at his chest.

The bartender made a grab at the sawed-off shotgun under the bar, and Kilkenny took him with his left-hand gun, getting off two shots. A third man let out a yelp and went out the front door, fast.

Jaime Brigo sat very still, his chair tipped back against the wall. He just watched Kilkenny, his eyes expressionless.

Kilkenny reloaded his pistols.

"Brigo," he said abruptly, "there are some men among us who would harm the *señorita*. Lem Calkins, and his brothers and sons. They would burn this place, and kill her. You savvy?"

"*Sí, señor.*"

"I must go up on the cliff. You must watch over the *señorita*."

Jamie Brigo got up. He towered above Kilkenny, and he smiled. "Of course, *señor*. I know *Señor Calkins* well. He is a man who thinks himself a good man, but he is cruel. He is also dangerous, *señor*."

"If necessary, take the *señorita* away. I shall be back when I have seen the man on the cliff."

The firing was increasing in intensity.

"You have seen Steve Lord?" Kilkenny asked Brigo.

"*Sí*. He went before you to the cliff. The *señorita* would not see him. He was very angry, and said he would return soon."

Kilkenny walked to a point just inside the window of the bar and out of line with it. For a time he studied the street. The bulk of the outlaws seemed to be holed up in the livery stable, and they were throwing out a hot fire. Some of the defenders were firing from the pile of stones beyond the town, and others from the bunkhouse. There was no way to estimate their numbers.

Some of the attacking party had closed in and got into position where they could fire into the face of the building. But for a time at least it looked like a stalemate.

Walking to the back door of the bar, Kilkenny slipped out into the yard and walked over to Buck. Safely concealed by the bar building, he was out of the line of fire of the defenders. Suddenly he heard a low call and, glancing over, saw Nita standing under the roses. An instant he hesitated, then walked over, leading Buck. For a moment he was exposed, but appeared to get by unseen.

Briefly he told her of Lem Calkins. She nodded.

"I expected that. He hates me."

"Why?" Kilkenny asked.

"Oh, because I'm a woman, I think. But he came here once, and had to be sent away. He seemed to think I was somewhat different than I am."

"I see."

"You are going to the cliff?" Her eyes were wide and dark.

"Yes."

"Be careful. There are traps up there, spring guns, and other things."

"I'll be careful."

He swung into saddle and loped the buckskin away, keeping the buildings between him and the firing.

When he cleared her house, a shot winged past him from the stone pile, but he slipped behind a hummock of sand and let the buckskin run. He was going to have to work fast.

Skirting the rocks, he worked down to the stream and walked Buck into it, then turned upstream. The water was no more than a foot deep, flowing over a gravel bottom, clear and bright. For a half mile he walked the horse upstream, then turned up on the bank, and followed a weaving course through a dense thicket of willows that slowly gave way to pine and cedar. After ten minutes more of riding, he rode out on a wide plateau.

Using a high, thumb-shaped butte for a marker, he worked higher and higher among the rocks until he was quite sure he was above and behind the cliff house. Then he dismounted, and dropped the bridle over Buck's head.

"You take care of yourself, Buck," he said quietly. "I've got places to go."

Leaving his carbine in its scabbard, he left the horse

and walked down through the rocks toward the cliff edge.

The view was splendid. Far below he could see the scattered houses of Apple Cañon, all of them silent in the morning sun. There were only a few. Around the cluster of buildings that made the town, there were occasional puffs of smoke. From up here he could see clearly what was happening below. The defenders were still holding forth in the livery stable and bunkhouse, and apparently in Sadler's house. His own attacking party had fanned out until they had a line of riflemen across the pass and down close to the town. They were fighting as the plan had been, shrewdly and carefully, never exposing themselves.

Kilkenny had worked out that plan himself. He was quite sure from what he had learned, and from what Rusty and a couple of others who knew Apple Cañon had told him, that the well across from Nita's house was the only source of water. That one bucket was empty, he knew, for it lay there beside the well, and alongside of it the gun that had fallen from the man's hand after Kilkenny had shot him. There were a lot of men defending Apple Cañon, and it was going to be a hot day. If they could be held there, and kept from getting water, and, if during that time he could eliminate Royal Barnes, there would be chance of complete surrender on the part of the rustlers. He believed he could persuade Steele and Frame to let them go if they surrendered as a body and left the country. His only wish was to prevent any losses among his own men while breaking up the gang.

Suddenly, even as he watched, a man dashed from the rear of the bunkhouse and made a run for the well and the fallen bucket. He was halfway to the well before a gun spoke. Kilkenny would have known that gun in a million. It was Mort Davis who was firing.

The runner sprawled face down in the dust. That would keep them quiet for a while. Nobody would want to die that way. It was at least 600 feet to the floor of the valley from where Kilkenny stood. Remembering his calculations, he figured it would be at least fifty feet down to the cliff house and the window he had chosen. Undoubtedly there was an exit back somewhere not far from his horse, or at least somewhere among the boulders and crags either on top or behind the cliff. There had to be at least two exits. But there wasn't time to look for them now.

He had taken his rope from the saddle, and now he made it fast around the trunk of a gnarled and ancient cedar. Then he dropped it over the cliff. Carefully he eased himself over the edge and got both hands on the rope. Then, his feet hanging free, he began to lower himself. His hands gave him no trouble.

He was halfway down when the first shot came, followed by a yell. The shot was from the livery stable, and it clipped the rock wall he was facing. His face was stung with fragments of stone.

Immediately his own men opened up with a hot fire, and he lowered himself a bit more, then glanced down looking for the window. He saw it. A little to the right.

Another shot clipped close to him, but obviously whoever was shooting was taking hurried shots without proper aim or he would not have missed. He was just thanking all the gods that the men behind the stone pile hadn't spotted him when he heard a yell, and almost instantly a shot cut through his sleeve and stung his arm. Involuntarily he jerked, and almost lost his hold. Then, as bullets began to spatter around him, he found a foothold on the window sill, and hurriedly dropped inside.

Instantly he slipped out of line with the window and froze. There was no sound from inside. Only the rattle of rifle fire down below.

The room he was in was a bedroom, empty. It was small, comfortable, and the Indian blankets spread on the bed matched those on the wall. There was a crude table and a chair.

Kilkenny tiptoed across the room and put his hand on the knob. Then slowly he eased open the door.

A voice spoke.

"Come in, Kilkenny!"

XVIII

Quietly Kilkenny swung the door open and stepped into the room, poised to go for a gun.

A man sat in a chair at a table on which there was dish of fruit. The man wore a white shirt, a broa leather belt, gray trousers that had been neatly pressed, and were tucked into cowhide boots. He also wore crossed gun belts and two guns. He was clean shaven except for a small mustache, and there was a black silk scarf about his neck. It was Victor Bonham.

"So," Kilkenny said thoughtfully, "it's you."

"That's right. Bonham or Barnes, whichever you prefer. Most people call me Royal Barnes."

"I've heard of you."

"And I've heard of you."

Royal Barnes stared at him, his eyes white and ugly. There was grim humor in them, too. "You're making trouble for me again," Barnes said.

"Again?" Kilkenny lifted an eyebrow.

"Yes. You killed the Webers. They were a bungling lot, but they were kinfolk, and people seem to think I should kill you because you killed them. I expect that's as good a reason as any."

"Mebbe."

"You were anxious to die, to come in that way."

"Safer than another way, I think," Kilkenny drawled.

Royal Barnes's eyes sharpened. "So? Somebody talks, do they? Well, it was time I got new men, anyway. You see, Kilkenny, you're a fool. This isn't going to stop me. This is merely a setback. Oh, I grant you it is going to cause me to recruit a new bunch of men. But this will rid me of some of your men, too. Some of the most dangerous men in the Live Oak country will be killed today. The next time, it will be easier. And, you see, I intend to come back, to reorganize, and to carry on with my plans. I'd have succeeded already but for you. Steele will fight, but if he isn't killed today, I'll have him killed within the week. The same for Frame and your friend, Gates. Gates isn't dangerous alone, but he might find someone else to work with, someone as dangerous as you."

The sound of firing had grown in tempo now, but Royal Barnes did not let his eyes shift one instant. He was cool, casual, but wary as a crouched tiger. In the quiet, well-ordered room away from the confusion below, he seemed like someone from another world. Only his eyes showed what was in him.

"You seen Steve Lord?" demanded Kilkenny.

"Lord?" Barnes's eyes changed a little. "He never comes here."

"He worked with you," Kilkenny flatly accused.

Barnes shrugged carelessly. "Of course. I had to use what tools I could find. I held Nita out to him as bait, and power. I told him I would give him the Steele Ranch. He is a fool."

Slowly Kilkenny reached for cigarette papers and began building a smoke, his fingers poised and careful. "You're wrong, Barnes. Steve is crazy. He's crazy with blood lust and a craving for power. He killed Des King. He killed Sam Carter and a half dozen other men. Now he's gunnin' for you, Barnes."

Royal Barnes sat up. "Are you tellin' the truth?" he demanded. "Steve Lord killed those men?"

Kilkenny quietly told him of all that had transpired

Outside, the shooting had settled to occasional shots, no more. A break was coming, and the tension was mounting with every second.

"Now," Kilkenny added, "if you want my hunch, I think Steve figgers to get you. He figgers with you gone, he'll be king bee around here."

Royal Barnes got up, and, for a moment, he stood listening.

"Somebody's on the trail now," he said suddenly.

That would be Steve. Instantly it came to Kilkenny with startling awareness that Barnes was waiting for something, some sound, some signal. If there was a spring gun on the main trail, it would stop Steve in his tracks.

He drew deeply on his cigarette. Somewhere he could hear water dripping slowly, methodically, as though counting off the seconds. Royal Barnes dropped a hand to the deck of cards on the table, and idly riffled them. The spattering sound of the flipping cards was loud in the room.

A heavy crash sounded again. That would be Mort Davis. Somebody else trying to get water. Somebody who wouldn't try again.

Gravel rattled on the trail, and Kilkenny saw Royal Barnes's face tighten.

Then in the almost complete silence: *Bang!*

Royal Barnes dropped into a crouch and went for his gun with a sweeping moment. At the same instant, he dumped over the table and sent it crashing toward Kilkenny.

Kilkenny sprang aside barely in time to escape the table, and a shot crashed into the wall behind him. His own gun was out, and he triggered it twice with lightning-like rapidity. Through the smoke he could see Royal Barnes's eyes blazing with white light, and his lips parted in a snarl of killing fury.

Then the whole room was swept up in a crashing roar of guns. Something hit him and he was smashed back against the wall. His own guns were bucking and leaping in his hands, and he could see bright orange stabs of flame shot through with crimson streaks. He stepped forward and left, then again left, then back right, and moving in. Barnes had sprung backward through a doorway, and Kilkenny crossed the room, thumbing cartridges into his six-guns.

He went through the door with a leap. A bullet smashed the wall behind him and another tugged sharply at his sleeve. He stepped over, saw Barnes, and fired. The flame blossomed from Barnes's gun and Kilkenny felt his legs give way as he went to his knees. Barnes was backing away, his eyes wide and staring.

Slowly, desperately Kilkenny pulled himself erect and tried to get a gun up. Finally he did, and fired again but Barnes was gone. Stumbling into the next room, he glared about. He was sick, felt himself weaving on his feet, and blood was running into his eyes.

The room was empty. Then a shot crashed behind him. He turned in a loose, stumbling circle and opened up with both guns on a weaving target. The he felt himself falling, and he went down, hard.

He must have blacked out briefly, for when he opened his eyes he could smell the acrid smell of gunpowder, and it all came back with a rush. He turned over, and drew his knees under him. Then, catching the door frame, he pulled himself erect.

Royal Barnes, his face bloody and ugly, was propped against the wall opposite, his lips curved back in a snarl. A bullet had gone through one cheek, entering below the nose and coming out under the ear lobe. Blood was flowing down his side. Blood was soaking his shirt, too. Barnes was cursing slowly, monotonously, horribly.

"You got me," he mouthed viciously, "but I'm killin' you, too, Kilkenny."

His gun swung up, and Kilkenny's own guns bucked in his hands. He saw Barnes wince and jerk, and the bloody face twisted in pain. Then the outlaw lunged out from the wall, staggering forward, his guns roaring a crescendo of hatred as he reeled toward Kilkenny. His shooting was wild, insane, desperate, and the shots went every which way.

He was toe to toe with Kilkenny when Kilkenny finished it. He finished it with four shots, two from each gun, at three-foot range, pumping the heavy .45 slugs into the outlaw. Barnes fell, and tumbled across Kilkenny's feet.

For what seemed a long time, Kilkenny stood erect, his guns dangling, empty. He stood staring blankly above the dead man at his feet, staring at the curious pattern of the Indian blanket across the room. He could feel his breath coming in great gasps, he could feel the warm blood on his face, and he could feel his growing weakness.

Then suddenly he heard a sound. He had dropped one of his guns. Abruptly he let go everything and fell headlong to the floor, lying there across Royal Barnes, the warm sunlight falling across his bloody face and hair. . . .

A long, long time later he felt hands touching him, and felt his own hand reaching for his gun. A big man loomed over him, and he was trying to get his gun up when he heard a woman's voice, speaking softly. Something in him listened, and he let go the gun. He seemed to feel water on his face, and pain throbbing through him like a live thing. Then he went all away again.

When he finally opened his eyes, he was lying on a wide bed in a sunlit room. Outside there were lilacs and he could hear a bird singing. There was a flash of red, and a redbird flitted past the window.

The room was beautiful. It was a woman's room quiet, neat, and smelling faintly of odors he seemed to remember from boyhood. He was still lying there when a door opened and Nita came in.

"Oh, you're awake." Nita laughed, and her eyes grew soft. "We had begun to believe you'd never come out of it."

"What happened?" he mumbled.

"You were badly hit. Six times, in all. Only one of them serious. Through the body. There was a flesh wound in your leg, and one in your shoulder."

"Barnes?" Kilkenny asked quickly.

"He's dead. He was almost shot to pieces."

Kilkenny was quiet. He closed his eyes and lay still for a few minutes, remembering. In all his experience he had never known any man with such vitality. He rarely missed, and even in the hectic and confused battle in the cliff house he knew he had scored many hits. Yet Royal Barnes had kept shooting, kept fighting.

He opened his eyes again. "Steve Lord?"

"He was killed by a spring gun. A double-barreled shotgun loaded with soft lead pellets. He must have been killed instantly."

"The outlaw gang?"

"Wiped out. A few escaped in the last minutes, but not many. Webb Steele was wounded, but not badly. He's up and around. Has been for three days."

"Three days?" Kilkenny was incredulous. "How long have I been here?"

Nita smiled. "You've been very ill. The fight was two weeks ago."

Kilkenny lay quietly for a while, absorbing that. Then he remembered.

"But Calkins?"

"He was killed. Jaime killed him, and two of his family. Steele put it up to the other Calkins boys to leave me alone and to leave Jaime alone or fight him and all the ranchers. They backed down."

The two weeks more that Kilkenny spent in bed drifted by slowly, and at the end he became restless, worried. He lay in Nita Riordan's bed in her house, cared for by her, and receiving visits daily from Rusty and Tana, from Webb Steele, Frame, and some of the others. Even Lee Hall had come by to thank him. But he was restless. He kept thinking of Buck, and remembering the long, lonely trails.

Then one morning he got up early. Rusty and Tana had come in the night before. He saw their horses in the corral when he went out to saddle Buck.

The sun was just coming up and the morning air was cool and soft. He could smell the sagebrush and the mesquite blossoms. He felt restless and strange. Instinctively he knew he faced a crisis more severe than any brought on by his gunfight. Here, his life could change, but would it be best?

"I don't know, Buck," he said thoughtfully. "I think we'd better take a ride and think it over. Out there in the hills where the wind's in a man's face, he can think better."

He turned at the sound of a footstep, and saw Nita standing behind him. She looked fresh and lovely in a print dress, and her eyes were soft. Kilkenny looked away quickly, and cursed himself under his breath for his sudden weakness.

"Are you going, Kilkenny?" she asked.

He turned slowly. "I reckon, Nita. I reckon out there

in the hills a man can think a sight better. I got things to figger out."

"Kilkenny," Nita asked suddenly, "why do you talk as you do? You can speak like an educated man when you wish. And you were, weren't you? Tana told me she picked up a picture you dropped once, a picture of your mother, and there was an inscription on it, something about it being sent to you in college."

"Yes, I reckon I can speak a sight better at times, Nita. But I'm a Western man at heart, and I speak the way the country does." He hesitated, looking at her somberly. "I reckon I better go now."

There were tears in Nita's eyes, but she lifted her head and smiled at him.

"Of course, Kilkenny. Go, and if you decide you want to come back . . . don't hesitate. And, Buck"—she turned quickly to the long-legged horse—"if he starts back, you bring him very fast, do you hear?"

For an instant, Kilkenny hesitated again, then he swung into saddle.

The buckskin wheeled, and they went out of Apple Cañon at a brisk trot. Once he looked back, and Nita was standing where he had left her. She lifted her hand and waved.

He waved in return, then faced away to the west. The wind from over the plains, fresh with morning, came to his nostrils, and he lifted his head. The buckskin's ears were forward, and he was quickening his pace.

"You an' me, Buck," Kilkenny said slowly, "we

ain't civilized. We're wild, and we belong to the far, open country where the wind blows and a man's eyes narrow down to distance."

Kilkenny sat sideward in the saddle and rolled a smoke. Then his voice lifted, and he sang:

I have a word to say, boys, only one to say,
Don't never be no cow thief, don't never ride no stray.
Be careful of your rope, boys, and keep it on the tree,
But suit yourself about it, for it's nothing at all to me!

He sang softly, and the hoofs of the buckskin kept time to the singing, and Lance could feel the air in his face, and a long way ahead the trail curved into the mountains.

Center Point Publishing
600 Brooks Road ● PO Box 1
Thorndike ME 04986-0001 USA

(207) 568-3717

US & Canada:
1 800 929-9108
www.centerpointlargeprint.com